HARVEY DUCKMAN PRESENTS...
VOL. 9

A collection of sci-fi, fantasy, steampunk and horror short stories

6e

Published in paperback in 2022 by Sixth Element Publishing

Sixth Element Publishing
Arthur Robinson House
13-14 The Green
Billingham TS23 1EU
www.6epublishing.net

© Sixth Element Publishing 2022

ISBN 979-8-442254-31-0

All rights reserved. No part of this publication may be reproduced, stored in a retrieval system or transmitted, in any form or by any means, electronic, mechanical, photocopying, recording and/or otherwise without the prior written permission of the publishers. This book may not be lent, resold, hired out or disposed of by way of trade in any form, binding or cover other than that in which it is published without the prior written consent of the publishers.

The authors assert the moral right to be identified as the authors of this work.

These works are entirely a work of fiction. The names, characters, organisations, places, events and incidents portrayed are either products of the author's imagination or used in a fictitious manner. Any resemblance to actual persons, living or dead, or actual events is purely coincidental.

CONTENTS

FOREWORD 1

THE LEGEND OF THE DOP A GLOP 3
by John Holmes-Carrington

LONELY HOPE by Graeme Wilkinson 25

TWENTY-SEVEN by Mark Hayes 30

DOWN AMONG THE DEAD MEN 46
by R. Bruce Connelly

SUPER BARRIO MOTHERS by Will Nett 63

THE FLATMATE by Davia Sacks 75

THE RAT IN THE DRAIN by Peter James Martin 83

ON A SILVER PLATTER by Robin Moon 99

BREAKING THROUGH by Joseph Carrabis 109

THE ROYAL INVENTION by A.L. Buxton 121

FUNGAL ROCK by C.K. Roebuck 149

HELL'S FALLS by Liam Hogan 167

THE EAGLE'S FLIGHT by Kate Baucherel 180

TULLY AND THE ASSASSIN by Liz Tuckwell 194

SHAMBLE by Ben Sawyer 209

FOREWORD

Welcome stranger,

Please, don't stand there on the step in trepidation… come in out of the cold. Let me take your hat and coat while you make yourself comfortable by the hearth.

I shall be just a moment, and please do forgive any unusual sounds you hear from within the walls. We've been having dreadful issues with our plumbing recently.

What's that? It sounds like faint screaming, you say. I assure you, it is just water, or at least some form of liquid, they tell me, gurgling through those ancient pipes. And the smell? Well yes, the plumber is working on that now, although when I think on it, I haven't seen him for a few days. Not since he went to check the old boiler in the basement.

Still, let's not let that spoil this time we have together.

I can tell you are a person of exquisite taste, so let me present to you the ninth in the series of eponymously titled, collected works of intrigue, fascination and wonder from a host of writers who are themselves as intriguing, fascinating and wonderful as the tales they weave.

Although I must also give warning, as writers are an odd bunch, who often have the strangest sense of humour… when I mentioned in passing that Duckman

Towers was having a minor plumbing issue, they took it upon themselves to submit a veritable literary smorgasbord of stories around a similar theme. I'm sure you'll soon see what I mean as you plumb the depths of this collection.

Meanwhile, I'm just popping out, so put your feet up, grab yourself a drink and enjoy our humble hospitality, and I'm sure by the time I return, and you have unclogged your imagination and flushed away any inhibitions, we will be strangers no longer, but the very best of friends.

Oh… and if you happen to see the plumber… well, let's just hope you don't.

Until next we meet.

Harvey

THE LEGEND OF THE DOP A GLOP

JOHN HOLMES-CARRINGTON

Some folk will wish, it's not that rare
For eyes a shining just like stars
For heads of full and lustrous hair
And skin silk-smooth and free of scars
Hear now my tale and heed it well.
I'll warn th' unwary and won't stop
I've pledged my life all folk to tell
The legend of the Dop a Glop

For I must warn you, vain of eye
Do not, I plead, down this road go.
There is a cost that's much too high
For teeth that gleam and cheeks that glow,
That is not paid by gold and jewel
But with a fee that does not stop.
Unless you heed me know that you'll
Forever pay the Dop a Glop

When bathing, take the utmost care
When letting out the water, run
Be sure to bind and stop your ear
Especial after setting sun
False offers rising from the drain
They'll promise. Yet just make them stop,
Else gain you everlasting pain
But pleasure for the Dop a Glop.

Do not so wish to change your skin
With offered 'dornment or attire.
Be thus content with that you're in
To snare the one, your heart's desire.
Tis well enough to have your health.
And your own will, don't ever swap.
Keep freedom now to be yourself,
Reject the charm of Dop a Glop!

"Oh, tell him to please shut up!" shouted a voice from the bathroom. "I've heard this tale every year for the last ten years!"

Startled, Marina, the young Ladies' Maid, heaved the shutters closed, hastily drew the drapes cutting the bard's tones off immediately and scurried back through to where her mistress was lounging in the bath.

Princess Alannah lay stretched out, staring as the water swirled around her legs. The bathwater, brown with the mud she'd washed off, eddied and lapped up the sides of the bath. She waggled her toes, watching the grubby ripples rebounding off the sides. As she flexed and bent her knees, the level swished up higher. She wondered briefly how high she could get it, but paused, arguing with herself as to whether trying would in the end launch the water over the side.

Marina coughed lightly to attract her attention.

"It's time to get out, M'lady." She spoke lightly, trying not to offend. It was never easy to tell what mood the princess would be in. Especially today. Backing away quickly, Marina silently laid out the large towel on a chair and scurried through to the dressing room shaking her head.

Alannah decided against launching the deluge across the bathroom floor and eased her leg back down gently with a minimal splash. She was in enough trouble as it was.

She'd been out enjoying the sights of the castle garden for most of the day teasing Lindel, the gardener's apprentice. She seemed to have brought a load of the garden back inside with her. Well, the muddier bits of it anyway. Marina had despairingly run the bath for the second time that day and aided her mistress, albeit unceremoniously as Alannah was a good head taller, into the comforting warmth.

Alannah didn't mind. She liked being in the garden, digging in what her father, the King, called their 'Royal Flower Patch' against the south rampart wall, but which resembled more of a rough lumpy scrub. It was still a definite work in progress despite his and the gardeners' enthusiasm, but it reminded him of his Queen.

Whenever she was in the garden, the princess adored the feeling she got with the clods of earth clinging heavily to her fingers as she pushed her hands into the wet sticky ground. Pulling back, she brought up great lumps that she could break up by rolling them between her hands. Besides, she liked to be different. All around her the courtiers were well dressed, highly polished in their great dresses and suits, but not Alannah. She liked wearing her earth tones, literally.

Princes Alannah was a tom boy, or 'Tom Girl' as she preferred to call herself. Ever since she had been able to walk, she'd been in trouble. Not malicious trouble. It was just that awkward things happened to her that usually ended up with something or someone getting broken, bent, injured, bashed or at the minimum, generally inconvenienced. Stuff just happened to Alannah. She sometimes wondered if she was jinxed.

The trouble frequently involved water. Several times she had needed to be rescued from the castle well. The last time she'd spent an entire afternoon sitting all the way down in the wooden bucket bobbing on the water at the bottom. Only when the Kitchen Maid came to draw water to prepare for the evening meal had they found her. Alannah swore that all she'd been trying to do was swing the bucket from one side to the other when the ratchet had given way and sent her plummeting. She'd found the descent exhilarating and was thoroughly disappointed when her father forbade her to ever do it again.

Yes, Alannah liked the mud, but she also had a thing for

the baths that followed. In fact, unusually for a child of her age, she loved baths. Any excuse she could generate to get back in was worth the reproaches from her frustrated parent. Many of her friends shared stories of how they had managed to escape the dreaded wash and scrub up so beloved of their respective responsible adults, but not Alannah. She actually 'enjoyed' bathing. She believed she had inherited the love at an early age sitting beside her mother, the Queen, as she herself luxuriated in the enveloping warmth.

Queen Helena had been well known for her beauty. The King had fallen for her looks at first glance, which was in itself odd, as he had been known for his 'somewhat picky nature' and many of his advisors had thought their ruler would pass out his days a bachelor. She was also well known for the time she spent perfecting it in the Royal Bathroom.

Alannah lazily scrubbed the remains of the garden from her body and pulled at the plug to release the water, wrapping the chain between her toes and yanking hard upwards by flicking her leg.

It resisted at first, swollen and stuck into the hole with the heat of the water, but a further sharp tug pulled it free, and the water began to run down and away.

"Are you done now?" Marina called eagerly, frustrated at the lack of speed, but momentarily heartened by the movement. "Your father is waiting for you to go down to the feast. The guests are assembled and the proceedings well under way!"

"Yes, Marina, I'm just finishing up," Alannah called back testily, rolling her eyes. "I'm coming now."

Stretching her leg as far as she could without having to slide down the bath, she coiled the plug chain round the taps, weaving it in a loop around both the hot and the cold. She smarted, recoiling as the arch of her foot brushed the cold tap, sharply cool in contrast to the warm water.

Lying perfectly still, leg outstretched, she felt the water level drop. Her sides were becoming colder slowly by degrees as the warm water receded. She would have to move soon, or she'd get ill or something. Or at least that's what her father said. She wasn't sure she believed him, but it was best not to try his patience too far.

"Don't spend too long in there whilst the water goes down," he called up every time, as she ascended the stairs to the bath, "or you'll suffer for it."

She didn't plan to. But there was one more thing to do before she got out.

Unweaving the last of the chain from between her toes, she knelt up. Scooting forward on her knees on the slippery surface, she leaned over the plughole and peered down into the darkness below.

Closing her right eye, she leaned closer to the hole with her left. She bent further, gingerly lowering her face to the opening. She knew she was being brave. The blackness of the hole, dark and damp as it lay beyond the metal of the drain, scared her a little.

Alannah held her breath as she peered into the dark. Holding as still as she could, she rested, motionless, hand splayed onto the curve at the bottom of the bath, elbows bent to their extreme, listening intently as the last of the bath water slurped and gurgled past her legs, down into the pipes below.

She counted down silently in her head, "6... 5... 4... 3..." Nearly there, would it come again? "2... 1..."

As the last of the water ran downwards, she heard what she'd been waiting for:

"*Dop, dop dop, boppa, dop a glop!*"

Yes! That was it. It was the one day of the year when it happened. She paused, holding her breath, hanging on as the last of the water drained out below.

"Thank you!" she whispered into the plug hole, "I'll be back soon."

Grinning wildly, she heaved herself to her feet, then sitting on the roll top of the copper bath, swung them over the side and into the waiting slippers. Grabbing her towel from the chair, she ran into her bedroom to get changed and to head down to dinner.

Her father was waiting for her in the Banqueting Hall. He was staring intently at the 'Big Pot' as she called it that hung over the Great Fire off to one side. The one he always asked Cook to use to make their meal when his favourite 'Venison in a Red Wine and Chocolate Gravy' was involved. The one her mother had insisted they use for special occasions. Today was the one such day each year that the King counted as special enough to use it. The anniversary of her mother's disappearance.

On this one occasion, it was wheeled out to hang over the wood fire in the huge fireplace in the hall for guests to admire. The outside showed the streaks of years of smoke that stained it, and which resisted the efforts of the Kitchen Boy to remove. But there suspended from the wrought iron arm, Cook would swing it out and back, the glorious aromas wafting out from it and around the hall, reminding the guests that the wait would be worth it.

Alannah scurried as quickly as she could through the great arch and into the Banqueting Hall. Pausing with as much decorum as she could muster, which wasn't a great deal given the haste with which she performed it, she curtseyed politely to her father before plonking herself on the chair to the right of his throne.

The Bard was finishing his annual recitation, bowing and receiving his applause.

"Hi Poppet." The King smiled, relieved that she had at last put in an appearance. "Did you have a nice bath?"

Alannah, paused, looking down the hall. The Bard had stopped and was staring hard at her, when he abruptly left.

"Yes, thanks," she replied distractedly, reaching up to quickly place a peck on his cheek. She sat down, peering round hungrily at the pan. "What are we having?"

"You know what we're having!" he chided. "It's Mother's celebration special, Venison in Red Wine and Chocolate Gravy. All these lovely people have come to join us." He waved his hand vaguely at the assembled dignitaries and glanced absently at the empty throne on his left, as if expecting to see his wife there.

Alannah winced at his momentary forgetfulness, but she too wished that her mother had still been sitting there. But then this was the reason for the annual feast. The same one they'd been having for ten years now.

It was more than ten years since her mother had 'disappeared' as her father called it. Alannah suspected that really, she was dead, and he didn't want to tell her. She might have been only very young at the time it had happened but having spent so much time out in nature with Lindel, she understood about the cycle of living things: birth, death and so on. Even at that age there are some things that a young head just knows.

Her father had tried to break the news gently to her and sugar the pill, but he'd found it difficult to explain to her what had happened. In fact, no one would ever say what had occurred. All they would confirm was that one evening her mother had gone up for a bath. She'd been a while and when the Maids had gone in to check on her the plug was out, and the water gone. So was the Queen.

The story of how her parents had first met was legendary in the Kingdom. For many years, the King had resisted all his suitors' attempts, or those of their doting fathers anyway, to catch his eye and have him choose them as his Queen.

Over thirty years of Grand Balls and Masquerades had passed with not a single eligible Lady even gaining a second chance. Let alone being invited back for further 'inspection' from His Majesty. Some of the more enlightened amongst his counsel had suggested that maybe they invite some eligible Men instead, but this didn't do the trick either. It seemed he was destined to remain celibate and alone.

Helena, however, was determined that she could turn his head.

In true portentous tradition, it had been a wildly stormy evening, with the weather trying its hardest to force its way into the Castle when she arrived. Most of the residents had braced the shutters against the torrent outside and bedded down for the night. The Guards were patrolling the battlements and the Door Warden had secured the Great Gates and was preparing to hunker down by the fire in the guardroom with a jug of ale. He had just taken his first sip when he heard the sound of hammering from just beyond. The gates themselves were over a foot thick and for the sound to penetrate it had to be loud.

Summoning the guard to join him, they dashed down to the Great Gate and paused, undecided. Despite the fortified nature of the Castle, it had been centuries since they had endured an attack and frankly, they were more than a little unsure of the next steps. The hammering came again.

Carefully opening the wicket gate, the Door Warden peered out. He was greatly relieved to discover not a large marauding horde but a woman in rain-soaked garments seeking shelter for the night. Thankful, he summoned her through.

The young woman paused, looking briefly back over her shoulder and stepped inside. The Door Warden, puzzled, stared out again into the night, but seeing nothing, shrugged and refastened the doorway.

The visitor stood shivering, staring inwards towards the Great Keep.

"Who are you and what do you want?" the Door Warden asked sharply.

"My name is Helena and I have come to marry the King," she said simply.

"Not likely tonight," was the reply. "Or ever if he has his usual way," he muttered to himself. He shook his head wryly. If this young madam wanted to see the King, she would have to wait until morning. He would by now be blissfully asleep, warm and sheltered from the terrible night. Disturbing him at this time would not be an option.

"You can shelter here for the night and be on your way in the morning." He gestured vaguely across the courtyard and motioned to the Guards, "Accompany her to the Steward."

The Guards, excited to be doing something other than tramping backwards and forwards in the teeth of a storm, escorted her eagerly to the Guest Lodgings.

Handing their charge over to the care of the Steward and duty done, they returned gratefully to the warmth of the guardroom to dry out.

Taking one look at the bedraggled being in front of her, the Steward sighed and shooed her in. She was too tired, and it was too late to argue. Shoving a blanket into her hands, the Steward ushered her along to an empty room.

The next morning, Helena rose early to seek out the Steward.

"I wish to see the King," she said again. "I am here to become his Queen. That is where I belong."

The Steward smiled wearily, looking at her and studying her closely. She was attractive in a rough, raw kind of way but she looked anything but presentable to impress a King, let alone become his Queen. Her face was streaked from the previous night's rain. Her garments were travel-stained and mud-splattered, and her hair hung matted, limp and lank. Strands of straw from the bedding stuck out all over.

"You won't be the first to think the King would be interested in you, nor I suspect the last. Good luck to you, but you're wasting your time, my dear." She rubbed her chin, adding sadly, "As have so many before."

"I merely require a bath and that will suffice. Then he shall see me and make me his Queen."

Shaking her head, the Steward handed Helena soap and a towel and pointed her on her way to the communal baths.

Barely ten minutes had passed when she emerged, transformed. The pale morning light shone off her dark hair, now braided in long tresses. Her face, freshly scrubbed, glowed in the sunlight, her cheeks flushed with rubbing. Her clothing looked fresh and clean, all traces of her nightly travel absent. Smiling brightly, she radiated beauty.

Timing her moment to perfection, she stepped forward.

Every morning before breakfast, the King would take a tour around the Inner Bailey of the Castle and so it was that their first meeting was in the warm glow of that morning's sun in the Castle Gardens. Seeing her there in simple garments, yet radiant in the morning, he stopped, stock still, dumbstruck.

"My Lord." She curtseyed, smiling brightly.

His mouth flopped open, and he nodded, gesturing her to approach.

"Have you… have you eaten?" he stuttered. "Er, breakfast?"

Shaking her head, she linked her arm in his and accompanied him inside. The Steward watched on dumbfounded. Was she really the same woman he'd met the night before? And was he really their King?

The King was smitten. For once he was truly interested and despite the fears of his subjects who were by now quite used to being disappointed in such things, they were married within the month. They were more surprised however as to how long it was before Princess Alannah was born. Her mother still looked ever youthful, but it was over ten further years after she had married before a child arrived, and many had given up hope of seeing a Royal child. The Royal Family was now complete and lived together contentedly and peacefully within the Castle.

The peace however, was not to last and by the time Alannah was three, Helena was gone as quickly as she had arrived.

Alannah's love of bathing was a constant source of worry to her father. For ages after her mother's departure, he'd sat alongside her, watching intently. As if scared that somehow, she would meet the same fate. He'd not cried or tried to stop her, but she knew watching her splashing in the water was painful for him.

Eventually he'd stopped. She hadn't realised, but it was exactly a year to the day from her mother's disappearance. Maybe he'd been reassured that she was safe and wasn't going anywhere, or whether the pain of the memory was dulling, even he wasn't sure, but it no longer felt appropriate for him to sit and watch his daughter as she bathed.

That's when he started the 'Annual Remembering' Feast. Each year after, a selection of the great and good (and some not so good if they could get in) of the land were invited to share a meal in the Castle as a memorial to the missing Queen.

On each anniversary, the Banqueting Hall was decorated with the best tapestries and finest garlands. Great bowls were filled with flowers from the Queen's beloved Gardens, and the air was heavy with their perfumed scent. All the arches and niches were filled with enormous beeswax candles bringing warmth and light to the normally dark and gloomy space.

On such occasions, the Big Pot was filled with the famous Venison in Red Wine and Chocolate Gravy. The same meal the Royal Couple had insisted on as their wedding celebration. Each year, the King would sit at the High Table on the Royal Dais accompanied by the arrayed guests and his daughter, and drink to the memory of his beloved wife.

There would be music and merriment reminiscent of that which he and The Queen had enjoyed and as much laughter as they could muster in the circumstances. But before everything, there would be the Recitation by the Royal Bard.

For Alannah, this was the fly in the ointment and the reason she was often late to attend. The Recitation by the Bard was always the first item and as far as she was concerned, wholly inappropriate. Besides, his dreary verse always delayed the best bits: the fun and the feast.

Not that the Bard was bad at his job. In fact, he was actually quite entertaining for the rest of the year. On most other occasions, he usually managed to make her laugh with what were quite hilariously naughty references to the below stair goings on. It was just the annual dirge that really put a downer on things.

She was fairly sure that the tale the Bard recited every year was a reference to her mother, though she couldn't figure out how, and her father seemed oblivious to the whole message in the content. For that reason, whilst The King had his annual memorial feast, Alannah made sure she had a bath that day. Two if she could wangle it.

Her mother's disappearance in the Bathroom didn't bother Alannah one bit when she sat in that same bath. On the contrary, it gave her a connection: a link to the woman she'd only known for a few years. An awareness that her mother too had lain in the same bath brought comfort and a feeling of closeness. Besides, despite what the Bard said, she liked the sound he warned about.

It was on the evening of one such 'Annual Remembering' when Alannah was around five years old that she first heard them.

Their castle had always been full of strange noises. The creak as her father settled down onto the throne in the banqueting hall. The howl of the wind as it battered the worn, sturdy walls. The hiss and crackle of the fires in the grates that both fed and warmed them. The screech of the rooks as they settled in the rookery on the bank of the moat beyond the west wall.

This however was one she'd not heard before. Pulling the chain on the plug had allowed the water to rush away down the plughole. She delighted in the swirl as the water spun quickly round and down and she leaned forward to watch more closely. That's when she'd heard it. The sound faint like an echo from below:

"*Dop, dop dop, boppa, dop a glop!*"

Just the once. A distinct combination and it intrigued her.

Alannah wanted to hear it again. For weeks, she would ask repeatedly for a bath every evening, dirtying herself deliberately to ensure her father couldn't disagree. It was a chore for her Maid to heat the water, yet there was no repeat of the noise.

Each day Alannah peered down the drain as if it would

help her hear more clearly. Kneeling with only one eye open, she'd stare down into the dark searching for the source, straining to hear it again, but to no avail.

The absence of reply went on every day, yet undeterred, Alannah never got bored. Each evening she would wait for the sound. Each evening nothing. So, the ritual continued for many days, weeks and months.

Until one evening as the water rolled down the drain, she heard it again.

"*Dop, dop dop, boppa, dop a glop!*"

Astonished, Alannah couldn't help herself and flung her body, full-length along the bath to stare back down the hole but there was nothing to see. Elated, she had dried off and almost bounced down to that year's memorial feast.

This tenth year as usual the merriment had gone on well into the night and Alannah was weary by the time she retired to bed. Drifting off to the sounds of the music below, she began to dream. In it, she was walking through her chambers. Outside, the sky was dark and the room was lit dimly with candles.

As usual the bath had been run. The steam coiled its way up from the surface into the cool air of the room. Tendrils of moisture rising and spiralling to meet her as she crossed the rug on the floor to the copper tub.

Approaching, she heard the sound of movement. The lazy splashing of someone in the water. Turning, she recognised the faint figure of her mother lying in the bath.

Still in the dream, Alannah stood immobile, startled by the vison when the figure in the bath put out a hand to her, beckoning her close. Entranced, Alannah walked closer, reaching out to meet the familiar touch.

As Alannah drew close the vision's lips moved and a voice sang out, but not with that of her mother.

Hello young miss and how d'you do?
What is it we can do for you?
Grant you three wishes, maybe more!
Then she release whom you adore.

She whom we met an age gone by.

That was your mother long ago
With flawless looks that we'd bestow.
Despite her years, no crease or sag
No hollow cheek, no ageing hag.

Did snare a King and draw his eye.

This same we offer now my dear
To never age another year
The beauty and the belle of ball
And at their feet let suitors fall.

Release her now and see her face,

A small reward is all we ask
It is no major daring task
Just join with us and set her free
The one you most desire to see

Repay us now. Come take her place!

Startled, Alannah awoke suddenly, the image of her mother still vivid in her mind. The words reverberating in her head "*Repay us now. Come take her place, Repay us now, Repay!*"

Flying forward from her bed, she bounded into the bathroom. Her own tears soaked her face, blurring her vision. Reaching out to touch where she'd dreamed her mother had been, her hand brushed imagined smooth familiar skin. Skin she had not touched for over ten years. Skin that brought back memories of moments like this, of tenderness and love and above all beauty.

The outstretched hand reached up as if for hers and she grasped at it, pushing the figment against her cheek. Imagined long fingers caressed her face, tracing its shape down from the hairline to the tip of her chin. The forefinger following the line across the soft dimple, that so enthralled young Lindel.

Looking up, her mother smiled warmly at her, the dark eyes, deep pools drawing her in as they had when she had been a child. The warmth of the gaze enveloped her, and Alannah dropped to her knees. Her mother's face seemed to positively glow. Grabbing at the hand and pulling it to her softly, it seemed to coalesce and solidify. It was a familiar touch. The same one she remembered from years before. Alannah hadn't realised how much she missed her mother.

The rhyme repeated, echoing in her skull, crashing through the confusion: *"Release her now… come take her place, release her, release…"*. The fingers slowly took on more substance and she nuzzled them again.

"I'll do it!" she whispered, the pain of loss suffusing her whole body. She heaved great sobs, her speech staccato as her gulped breaths wracked her body. Then louder, "Release her." She was shouting now, "I'll do it. I'll take her place!"

The gentle hand turned, the fingertips stroking her face again then stopped as they brushed her own hand, pressing it against her own cheek. Alannah closed her eyes, lost in the moment. Yearning.

At that moment, the bathroom door crashed open. The King barrelled in followed closely by the Bard.

Viciously, the hand twisted, flashing round and snaring Alannah's wrist. Dragging tightly, pulling hard, yanking her off her feet, over the roll top and crashing her into the bath.

The pressure was relentless, and Alannah struggled for a moment as her face entered the water. Her windpipe closed, crushed in the steel grip of panic, she forced a silent, tormented bubbling scream.

Feeling herself being dragged slowly across the smooth base of the bath, she tried vainly to release the vice on her wrist. The plug was out, and the bath water began to recede, dragging her with it. Her vision darkened and she could smell only the harsh tang of copper. Her face pressed into the plughole, she faded through it into the long dark of the drain, pulled down by the water. The sound of it pouring mingled with laughter at the edge of her hearing as she fell downwards, endlessly sinking.

The King and the Bard leapt towards the bath as the fading image of his daughter drifted down, swirling into the plughole, the last vestiges of her nightdress twisting, spiralling as it descended out of sight.

Howling with rage, his face a mask of horror, the King lunged at the disappearing fabric, desperately stretching, trying to pull her back but his hand only grasped thin air and he collapsed.

He lay there, exhausted, panting as a soft hand touched his shoulder, long slim fingers gripping it gently, easing him back. He felt warm breath on his neck. And a low, familiar voice, "She should have listened to the Bard, and to you, my love. You did warn her."

The King half turned, amazed.

The face before him smiled the radiant smile that had captured his heart in the Castle Garden all those years ago. Kneeling, she kissed him. "Don't be alarmed, my love. I have returned."

Enchanted once more by the familiar unchanged face, the King could only stare as the seductive voice continued. "I am back again at your side for ever." He nodded as she continued, "Payment has been made and I am returned still beautiful, and I will be your Queen once more."

Her hand touched his head as he knelt. Wordlessly he took and kissed it, hopelessly smitten, oblivious to all else. His eyes bewitched, stared at the vision on front of him.

The Bard slowly headed towards the door, only turning briefly as the last vestiges of the bath water drained away. Shutting the door behind him, he left, shaking his head sadly,

As the door closed, a few tiny droplets ran over the edge of the plughole, trickling in mini rivulets into the darkness below. As the door clicked shut, he heard an echo, like an afterthought:

"*Dop, dop dop, boppa, dop a glop!*"

As a child, John Holmes-Carrington was once asked, "If you could do anything you wanted for ten minutes, what would you do?" He unhesitatingly replied, "I'd spend the time living in my own imagination." Now, many years later, he has discovered that Harvey Duckman Presents provides him with a fabulous way to achieve this for so much longer than just ten minutes.

LONELY HOPE
OR NO HOPE AT ALL...
IT'S ALL THE SAME TO ME

GRAEME WILKINSON

Yep, it's finally happened. I've finally become the embodiment of everything I've always hated. The epitome of everything I've always mocked. All those idiots and fools I've howled at have finally come back from the dead to well and truly bite me square on the arse. It's almost enough to inspire a quick death at the hands of a decent dollop of KMQ on the tip of the tongue. But no, I shall battle on. Just like I always do, but, yep… for now, I'm fucked. Drifting, helpless in space. I can see it out there now, all black and spinning past the window like a reputation going down the toilet. GH456XP-7 whirls by every three minutes exactly as well, a planet-sized face laughing its tits off at my expense.

Yep, go on… you laugh too… get it over with… for I, Lonely Hope, am now one of them. One of the poor sods that die wailing and moaning in outer space after making some rudimentary error in judgment. And, to make it even spicier, it's also my fucking birthday.

Thought you'd like that one, you sadistic bastard.

The life support died about an hour ago. Everyone else jumped into 'sleep but me, the fucking selfless heroic piece of dimwit that I am, stayed out to make sure they had a chance to actually come out of it.

Although, there only being six 'sleep pods for seven crew kind of helped too. As did losing the coin toss.

Not that it matters now, we'll all be dead soon enough.

I can't decide which is worse: me out here, knowing how fucked I am or them, in their pods, asleep and happily oblivious to their impending fuckedness.

Oblivion sounds glorious.

On the plus side, the ship's sound enough apparently. Big hole starboard but we managed to get it locked down before there was too much damage.

Thank heaven for small mercies, eh?

I suck in a deep breath and blow it out, aware that I probably shouldn't have done it.

"Liv," I say, "how long's left?"

An electronic squelch… that's Lividity, the ship, whirring into action. "There is," she says, "one minute and thirty-three seconds less air than there was the last time you asked. And talking is only going to use it up quicker. Now, will you leave me be while I try to figure us all a way out of this?"

I huff a bit. More for form's sake than anything else.

"Liv," I say, "you won't tell anyone about this, will you?"

"No," she says. "For the hundredth time, I will not tell anyone you ended up drifting in space, waiting to die like you're the punchline to a bad joke about… I don't know… a dead floater or something…"

I laugh in spite of myself. "A *what*…?"

"A dead… ah… fuck off." Another electronic squelch and she's gone.

"A… dead… floater…" I repeat, sniggering.

Ironically, the job had gone brilliantly. We were in and out like no one's business.

It wasn't an easy job, mind. None of our jobs are easy, but this one went like clockwork. The body was all in one piece, which is always helpful. There's nothing worse than slopping through an airlock with a head in one hand, an arm in the other and a torso tucked under your arm. I mean, the heavy work is usually down to Inch but sometimes his… erm… lack of brainpower can cause more problems than he's worth and it's best to just keep him out of the way. 'He's not very bright but he can lift heavy things' is the phrase, I think. Poor fucker is done for now though.

And he won't even know it.

I suppose I could wake them up. Let them die while they're awake. I don't reckon they'd thank me though.

Anyhow, the job went well, as I was saying. We'd been commissioned by some top end government official to recover the body of his wife. Her ship had mysteriously 'come apart' somewhere in the Yerval belt… he wasn't exactly sure where. Turns out the Yerval belt is fucking massive… an ever-expanding phenomenon is what they call it. An ever-expanding pain in the bum is more accurate, if you ask me.

Weirdly, finding the remains of the ship was easy…

the distress beacon was still flagging away like a screaming huji monky in a library. So Glunt took us in nice and close, and we slipped through the junk real sloopy.

And there she was… the wife. Just floating there.

Now, get this… she was totally nude except for a black sock on her right foot. We thought the foot had come off at first but then Roma spotted little tiny pink love hearts patterned over the thing.

She's got good eyes has my Roma. Good other things as well.

I'll not see her again though.

Fuck, I need a drink. Not going to happen that though. Not a drop of drink and all that.

We pulled the wife in and that was that. Job done. Well, half done. All we had to do then was hightail it out of there and drop her off at Von Hofmann's.

We were halfway there when things went wrong.

And oh how badly wrong they went.

I still can't believe it. I really, really can't believe it.

You know the weird feeling you get in that tiny, tiny instant when you do something and then you know you shouldn't have done it because it was stupid and it's definitely going to hurt? That awful sinking feeling?

Yep, I've been feeling that for a while now.

We thought we'd found another ship. Drifting.

Then we thought we'd click onto it and maybe see what we could salvage. We may be in the corpse recovery business but a bit of extra revenue never goes amiss.

Anyone would have done the same thing.

At least that's what I keep telling myself.
And now we're all going to die.

Graeme Wilkinson was born in County Durham in 1973 and left it as soon as he could. He managed to get all the way to Teesside. Which is not very far at all. He is the author of the Battenberg Trilogy of metaphysical, theological, intergalactic, time-travel, post-apocalyptic, dystopian, Dickensian, bizarro fest novels.

TWENTY-SEVEN

MARK HAYES

I was born on the 3rd of December 1833. I'd been aware of my existence for two months prior to my painful disturbing entry into the world, or for twenty-seven years, depending how you look at it.

It was on that early December morning I learned first-hand what a blessing it had been that I had no recollection of my previous birth. For I shall tell you this much, humans were never meant to be truly self-aware when we are born. Our births are traumatic enough for our mothers, traumatic enough for ourselves, without us being fully conscious of being pushed into the world.

You're confused, I know. You'll think me mad, and in truth there have been many occasions I have doubted my own sanity. But the 3rd of December 1833 was not my first birth and two months before that day, I died.

It was, as I remember, a particularly painful prolonged death. They had plied me with morphine but just enough to stop my screaming. It would have been a kindness for them to cut short my suffering with a blade to the throat, or to have smothered me with a pillow. Instead, they let me linger for days in silent agony from the fateful sabre wound that had near disembowelled me.

There was no solace to be had in that wound. It was not a wound taken in honour. I had been gutted in a pointless duel over an ill-advised insult, an insult I had given. I'd been drunk at the time, heady with perceived success. I'd been celebrating what I foolishly considered to be my artful seduction of a senior officer's wife.

In that life I was a cavalry man. In truth, no more than a lowly second lieutenant, but full of myself as such men so often are, without any real achievements to my name. That night, I was regaling my fellows in the regimental mess with the tale of my amorous adventures with an artillery major's wife. As I told it, to the hilarity of all, I believed, she was a woman with a firm little arse but a face only the blind would call pretty. I went further, as the laughter grew, making some off-colour remarks. You know the kind of thing.

Before you judge me, know only that I was a different person then. Literally in fact. In later lives I would come to hate the kind of man I had been. The kind of man who would say something like, "You don't look at the mantle while you're poking the fire."

Unfortunately, the man I was then was obliviously unaware the woman in question was the sister of a captain in my regiment. A captain sat but a table away from me and my rowdy compatriots, as I took things even further, profanely acting out of my amorous adventures for the benefit of my friends. If my 'friends' that night knew the captain was the lady's sibling, they did nothing to rein in my coarseness, nor did they warn me he had risen to his feet behind me, doubtless enraged. If they had, I suspect I would not have proclaimed that we should call her 'the regimental horse,' as not only I, but so many of my fellow officers in the King's 9th had taken a ride astride her.

That there was some truth in this does not lessen my guilt. Lady Gertrude had a thing for young horsemen, and a husband with no interest in her save her money. But while I was not alone in my conquest of the major's wife, I was the first man stupid enough to brag about doing so in the mess, in her brother's presence.

So it was I came by my pointless death in a pointless duel with Captain Hans Fredrick. A duel I agreed to flushed with youthful arrogance, an inflated sense of my own abilities, and a stomach full of wine. I wish I could claim it became a famous duel, epic in proportion, fought between two master swordsmen. I wish I could say that we fenced for hours, that it was ill-luck that caused the misstep that cost me my life. In truth, he knocked aside my sabre with ease and gutted me with a simple riposte. I remember clearly as he stood over me, his earlier rage giving way to disgust. He spat upon me as I lay in agony on a grassy lawn and walked away without giving me a second glance.

My cohorts dragged me to the infirmary, those bosom friends of mine. Dragged me through the doors and dumped me in a cot to die. Then doubtless returned to their drinks and perhaps a hand of cards. In the week it took me to die, not one of them visited me again. I dare say they knew my worth. I can't say I blame them.

The surgeon patched me up, but gangrene set in on the second day. Eating away at me from the inside. A slow painful ignominious death for 2nd lieutenant Arthur Maydew. A bitter end to a pointless unremarkable life. I would not have believed it at the time, but now I look back on Arthur's life I doubt even his father was much moved at the funeral of his third and most disappointing son. I wasn't there of course. Well, no more than anyone attends their own funeral. I was there in body, my spirit though had already moved on. I suspect it was a pathetic little gathering. Few tears shed by the few bothering to attend. But I doubt it matters, as I say, I was already elsewhere. Though nowhere anyone expects to find themselves after a painful slow death finally drags you to your end, saving the Buddhists and Hindus of this world. But even they do not expect to plunge from the agony of a gangrenous death straight into the dark smothering warmth of the womb, least ways not fully conscious of the life they have just so bitterly departed.

Sigmund Freud made much of the sanctuary of the womb. He would have it that we long to return to the safety and security that our subconscious remembers feeling as each of us floated in the darkness and warmth of utero. He would have it that we recall, deep within, a sense of wellbeing we can never recapture. That we long once again to feel the vibration and sound of our mother's heartbeat. It is because of this unconscious desire that we strive to return to such a state all our lives, driven by our very id to seek the impossible and recapture that nirvana that was the precious bond we felt with our mothers within the womb.

Sigmund was wrong, trust me on this, because having returned to the womb, believe me, nothing is quite so terrifying.

The moment of Arthur's passing, I passed into the blind half formed foetus that would house my next existence. In that realm of total sensory deprivation, I was overwhelmed by heat and vibrations. The dull resonant thud of my mother's heartbeat encompassed everything and it felt akin to drowning. You can trust me on that too… There is nothing reassuring about being in utero. Floating in utter darkness, at the mercy of the unknown, utterly helpless and utterly alone.

That said, being in utero is probably more reassuring if you're not self-aware. If you lack the recollection of departing the mortal coil in agony moments before. Added to which I knew I had led a less than saintly life. Combined with the knowledge of my own death, I remember feeling I was in some cruel purgatory that first time. I knew not what was happening to me. I was in the dark, both figuratively and literally. But I knew as Arthur Maydew I hadn't led an exemplary life.

Arthur had been raised in the Anglican tradition but he little cared for the church's doctoring of abstinence and good Christian values. The third son of a respectable family he'd wasted what few talents he'd been gifted on a string of pointless endeavours. When other avenues for advancement had been used up, he'd talked his father into funding a commission with horse guards. And why was that? Did he, the I that was, have some driving patriotic compulsion to serve his country? No, it was simply because he fancied himself in the uniform.

I was, not to put too fine a point on it, a drunken lout, a womaniser and a bully. I was a man who delighted in abusing what little power I possessed. The kind of officer who punishes the men under his command for the slightest infraction, perceived or real. I took pleasure handing out the worst punishments I could design and then took even more pleasure in bragging about it afterwards. In short, I was something of a shit and I knew it too. So, when I found myself floating in the darkness and heat of utero after my timely demise, well, I was convinced I was in hell. A hell I richly deserved.

And then, on the 3rd of December, I was born again, in the literal not religious sense.

That too led to its own strange purgatory.

To say I was a strange infant is an understatement. I was strange in that I knew who and what I was. Yet I was still an infant, with an infant's control over my bladder, an infant's control over my emotions, and an infant's ability to communicate those emotions. I was in fact as helpless as any other infant despite being aware of my previous life, I was also no more able to understand my mother's words than any other infant. My body was new for all my soul was old. I could not understand why this was but in time I came to understand a little about the chemistry of the brain. Neurons need to make the connections before what you hear becomes something you can understand. The same applies to speech and any other aspect of the physical. If anything, knowledge of my prior existence only made my new one harder.

My mother tried, like any mother, to calm her infant, but I screamed, flailed and struggled all the more.

In time, this new me was christened Brian Caine and I came to answer to that name. The memories of Arthur and aspects of his life became clouded like an adult's memories of childhood. Despite those memories, I had to relearn so much. Maths, science, language were concepts I learned anew. What I remembered of such things from my former life were broken echoes of another's past. In this new life I was a son of paupers, who I came to resent far more than their due. As Brian, I was put to work in a mill age six and schooled on Sundays with Methodist redemption between the alphabet and numbers. Those early years in the mills were hard and bred a bitterness within me born of Arthur. I had memories of an earlier life of privilege. I remembered too well the joys and arrogance of wealth. I came to believe the hardships of Brian's life were God's punishment for Arthur's misdeeds, but rather than being pushed by this towards piousness, I took the other road. Resentment, anger, bitterness… this was my creed. When of an age I took to drink, and with it, thievery. In a short time, Brian came to have even less to recommend him than Arthur. Perhaps that speaks to my character, that given a second turn of the wheel, I came out all the worse. As Brian grew older, so his crimes grew, and his bitterness with it. Eventually such a life will always catch a man up and in time it did. A drunken fight over a few shillings ended with a blade in the gut, another this time, not my own. But for that blade I was brought up before the beak, and the blade proved the death of me as surely as if it had been stuck in me. The man in the wig sentenced me to the gallows before the sunset on that day, the day after I had just turned twenty-seven for the second time.

The irony did nothing to sooth my bitterness, but as I walked to the gallows it occurred to me that was almost to the day the same age as Arthur had been when he lost his fateful duel. I remember making some acrimonious remark to the hangman, "Better luck in the next one then…" Of course, I had not known, I had not realised the truth of my existence, not then, as the trapdoor fell away and I dropped to Brian's doom as the rope around his neck snapped tight.

Twenty-seven… Years after Brian, Jimi Hendrix was to die at twenty-seven and so did Janice Joplin. They weren't alone. Jim Morrison, Brian Jones, Amy Winehouse, Kurt Cobain. Not to mention Robert Johnson, the father of the blues, who sold his soul to the devil at the crossroads. All dead at twenty-seven. Like Arthur, like Brian… There's something about that age, it's not just musicians that die at that age. Racing drivers, sportsmen, poets, kings, emperors… even popes. Three of them in fact, though the one that stands out is John XII, the pope who turned the Vatican into a brothel and died ignominiously from a fatal stroke whilst in bed with a married woman. God's judgement on his wayward priest some might say… How do I know this odd piece of trivia? Well, maybe I'm a little obsessed with the number twenty-seven, but then I was that age when gangrene took my life as Arthur and twenty-seven again in 1860 when as Brian I walked to the hangman's noose.

Seventeen years later in 1877, Richard Thwaite, a cobbler's son, left Doncaster and joined the army to avoid a life of nailing boots. Ten years passed and he'd done well, raised through the ranks to the giddy hights of sergeant. Richard was a pious man. He swore off strong drink, though he remembered the taste of ale and the joys of drunkenness from his other lives. He was well liked, though some thought him too soft on the men for a sergeant. But he was good at it, he remembered soldiering, all be it from astride horse and as a life it suited Richard. He was asked once by an officer why he was so forgiving of his men. He told the officer he was trying to be a better man, to make up for his past. Which was true, but not in a way the officer would ever have believed.

One hand on his rifle, and one hand on his bible, Richard Thwaite marched to the army's drum and tried to guide rough angry drunken louts to a better path. He felt he was doing the Lord's work as well as the Queen's, and he hoped in doing so he might break his curse. For he had become convinced this third life was his chance to rectify the black stains upon his soul that Arthur and Brian's lives had left…

Then just before he turned twenty-seven Richard, or rather I, was posted to Zululand as a new colony was founded. I thought little of it, the war was done, it was a peaceful little backwater. A few weeks later, not long after the anniversary of my third birth, there under a foreign sun, the regiment celebrated Queen Victoria's golden jubilee. I remember being happy, drinking tea while others drank to the Queen's health with stronger beverages, laughing with friends as the men fired off their rifles in salute to Her Majesty. I was still laughing at the drunk antics of the men when the bullet hit me.

It was an ignominious death all told. An accident. What odds would you lay a stray air-shot would whistle down and punch through heart and lung. Killing Richard dead in an instant. Killing me without giving me even a moment to regret my passing…

Back I went to the womb, that all too familiar purgatory. Floating in utero, with the memories of three lives and a number for company…

So, you'll forgive me if I became obsessed with the number twenty-seven when next I was born two months later in Calcutta. Born daughter of a house maid working for a British family. That then was a shock. First I saw my mother's light brown face, and then more so when I realised what was not between my legs.

That mother of mine came from Buddhist stock, rare but not unheard of in that part of India. She taught me her beliefs as she raised me, unaware that I had my own strange perspective upon them. She helped me though and as Brinda I came to terms a little with the oddity of my existence. Though life as an Indian girl in Calcutta at the turn of the century was complicated enough. More so for I remember lives as a man, and I was who I was. That I found hardest to reconcile, my predilection had not changed, and in those days, a woman attracted only to women was something the world did not accept. I fled India to avoid a marriage I did not want and became a nurse in a country I knew better than any would believe and hid who I was as best I could. But of my other lives and that damn number, I was reconciled by 1914 and when the war came, I volunteered to serve as a nurse behind the front lines. The Great War as we were calling it then. I knew what would be coming, as Brinda had reconciled with my fate. I almost welcomed her coming end, while I sought to ease the suffering of others and seek some karmic balance to my strange existence. All the stranger having lived a life as a her.

Though if Buddhism helped me reconcile to my fate, I was not so reconciled I did not feel terror the night the shells started to fall.

Twenty-seven years later, a midshipman named Alec was feeling a growing sense of dread as he stood upon a Hawaiian beach. Another life, a different nationality, a different service, but I knew something was coming as my birthday slipped past. Perhaps I could have warned them, but who would have listened to my warnings.

Alec's was a difficult life, growing up through the great depression. Son of an evangelist pastor, brought up on God and redemption, and believing in neither. Christ had no answers, nothing in the Bible explained my plight, and my father's belt was the only answer to any question I asked of him.

To escape the tyranny of a pious man and the poverty of the dust bowl, I'd joined the navy to see the world once more. I did well, as I always did, I'd come to like the military life. I was marked as a man who showed no fear, but it's easy not to fear when you know at twenty it's not your time to die. Though my fellow sailors found me strange at times when it came to talk of women. Not for me a leering glance or whistle as a girl walked past. I'd led a life on the other side of such things. A life that had given me a new perspective all around. I tried to treat each the same, no matter what hung, or not, between their legs, or the colour of their skin. But as twenty-seven came around in 1941, I wondered if Alec had made a difference in the lives of anyone, as I stood upon that beach, a little place called Pearl Harbour, and watched the zeros flying in. Well, I'm sure you can guess the rest.

Twenty-seven years later, it was the swinging sixties. Julie Sunburst, another sapphic life, but so different this time round. Julie burned her bra and freaked out to The Beatles and The Stones. I knew too well what would come at twenty-seven. I was doomed to die… Again, and again as that number rolled around. But there is a freedom in such a fate. I took risks, took drugs, and lived the wild child life. I was the queen of free love, the epitome of a flower child. I taught eastern spiritualism and the love of life to hippies and freaks in Frisco. The life of a woman in the sixties was freer than it had ever been. Freer than an Indian girl's at the turn of the century. And the drugs, oh the drugs. The wonder of LSD. I overdosed twice in 66 but wow what a trip that was. They called me wild, and wild I was…

But then…

Maybe it was a side effect of all the drugs, a hangover long overdue. Maybe I was just burnt out, too many lives lived, too many times rebooted… As the year turned in 68, a strange depression took hold of me. I came to believe in my soul that I wanted it all to end. I wanted to be done with my endless prolonged existence. I had no wish to face another life, to take another throw of the dice, another turn of the wheel. I got it in my head to end it all, to have an end so absolute that there could be no coming back this time. I hitched my way to Nevada, to join the protests outside of the boxcar tests.

Make love not war…

I chose a third way, I chose oblivion, and stole across the fences. I ran across the desert to embrace the bomb. To embrace that most unholy creation of the atomic age. I wanted an end to it all, an end of me. I wanted, no, needed, a final death, I sought it out. A final end to my prolonged existence beneath the mushroom cloud…

Nineteen-ninety-five and as a man, I was still alive.

Sarajevo, another battlefield, another war. Mankind

never learns and neither do I. It had come to me that humans are fated to keep repeating their mistakes, one generation to the next. The 60s gave me hope that the cycle might end, for all I ended them in despair. That was the generation who could have changed it all, so what the hell happened to them as they grew old. It made me thankful I never had. This time I'd been born in England once more, too late for punk, though I knew their rage. Thatcher's children sickened me, putting money ahead of common decency.

I joined the army once again, guess I don't learn either, but it's what I knew best. When in 95, twenty-seven rolled round once more, and I died to not one bullet but a score. Protecting a child, my body his shield. I hope he lived and the wounds of war would heal. I wondered then if sacrifice was the key, if my life for another's would set me free…

Which brings me to here, as I sit in this bar, talking to you. This latest life was much like the last. Now it's all but done with, all but the shouting. What have I learnt, over all these lives? I remember them all Arthur, Brian, Richard, Brinda, Alec, Sunbeam Starburst as Julie was known, Frankie the one who saved the life of a child and me, finally me, till the next one comes around. Yet I've nothing to share for all those lives, all those faiths. It's all still a mystery to me. And why twenty-seven? Who the hell knows. Ask Jimmy and Janis if you meet them, if they're still around.

I've sought out others, you see, over the years. Sought

people like me, living life after life. I found only frauds, hoodwinks and fools. So maybe we all follow the same path, maybe the souls of all of us come back. But if that's true then I've seen no proof of others and know only my own. So maybe it's just me or maybe us all, but if you're banking on answers, well, I have them not.

It's 2022 and it's been, well, a strange couple of years. I didn't fear the pandemic, not yet at least, but my birthday is coming and orders have arrived. Another war, another conflict, another opportunity to die. Another chance this might end, but I suspect it will not. Twenty-seven will destine me to the womb once again.

So, what have I learnt?

What do I know?

What advice can I give you, some great insight before I go?

Life's short, you should live it… unlike me, you may not get another go.

Author of the Hannibal Smyth Misadventures, The Ballad of Maybes series and his first two books, Passing Place and Cider Lane, Mark Hayes writes novels that often defy simple genre definitions; they could be described as speculative fiction, though Mark would never use the term as he prefers not to speculate. When not writing novels, Mark once had fleeting renown as a dancer on the shores of midnight and was born on the same day that Lovecraft died, though he swears these events are not related. He is also a 9 n'tupence Dan

Black Belt in the ancient Yorkshire martial art of EckEThump, favours black eyeliner and believes in a one man one vote system but has yet to supply the name of the man in question.

Mark has also been known to not take writing his bio very seriously.

Find out more at www.markhayesblog.com

DOWN AMONG THE DEAD MEN
(BEING THE SEVENTH CHAPTER OF THE BIKE CYCLE)

R. BRUCE CONNELLY

The graveyards were very busy on Sunday morning. One grave was being prepared to receive the earthly remains of Buddy Walsh, killed Friday night in a bicycle accident.

Another was being visited on that same bicycle over and over by Ted Henderson looking to see if a grave would appear with a warning device allowing someone prematurely buried to ring a bell.

The third graveyard hadn't been used in years, but would be in use this Sunday morning because who would think to look for the body of a man who had been killed in a plot he had bought and paid for years before in preparation for that eventuality?

Jeff awoke at dawn on Sunday, half-dressed and lying on the lawn. Next to him was what appeared to be a hollowed-out carcass without a head. The sight made him jolt back away from it, his hands skidding in the blood-saturated grass, causing him to fall face-forward into the eviscerated abdomen. He gagged in revulsion, shoving the corpse away from him as he vomited up a human finger. The sight caused him to vomit again and again until his stomach was emptied. He pushed himself to his knees, and then stood, dragging the back of his hand across his mouth. Blood. So much blood! Was he injured? He looked down at himself. Everything he could see was coated in red, his chest, his arms, his belly, startlingly swollen, his pants torn, muddy, and soaked in blood.

What had happened? Who was this lying on the lawn of the 300-year-old Peck homestead? His eyes slowly moved back to look at the finger he had regurgitated… and the gaudy, blocky ring still on that finger.

Alistair Peck.

He had vomited up Alistair Peck's finger which meant he had eaten much of Alistair Peck.

He threw a glance toward the barn and experienced another shock. Cars. In the driveway. Someone has arrived! No, someone *had*. Baldwin. Just before the moon rose on its second of three nights that caused such a startling change in Jeff's physiognomy. Twelve hours ago. Was Baldwin still…?

Jeff walked into the house following a trail of blood that marked Alistair's final exit from the family home. The doorway into the living room was open. It couldn't close because of what was left of Mr Baldwin.

There wasn't a lot left. A couple of arms and legs and

some of what was once a hand. Jeff spun, surprisingly quickly for a man of his girth, making it into the bathroom in two strides. He'd thought he'd emptied himself completely on the lawn but there were still some bits of Peck and Baldwin to expel. He flushed the toilet and to add to the horror, the water level *rose* instead of sinking. He quickly turned the handle on the wall to stop the water's flow and grabbed the plunger. Several strong pushes on the handle and the water and refuse gurgled out. He turned the water back on, tried to flush once more and the water again rose. Again, a twist of the handle and the flood was averted.

Perfect. Just perfect.

Jeff washed his hands, then his arms, then his hands again, the water running red down the sink's drain. He splashed water onto his chest, then his face, soaping himself frantically… so much blood… then realised he should just shower. Stripping off his torn jeans, he turned the water on full force and stepped into the shower stall, barely acknowledging the startling increase in the size of his belly since the day before. But when he did, and realised why, he retched once again, into the shower.

By the time he was satisfied, the bar of Lifebuoy was a mere sliver. He towelled off, tied the wet towel as best he could around his waist and stepped out of the bathroom. After the job he had in front of him, he would need another shower but at least he had removed most of the Baldwin/Peck remains from his hair and from beneath his nails.

Stepping over the body in the doorway, Jeff entered what looked like an abattoir. Blood covered the rug Letitia Peck had woven by hand in 1680. And speaking of hands, one lay like a dead spider on the hearthstone amidst rubble that had once been a rooster, a particularly hideous work of porcelain. On the mantel, at opposite ends, their eyes staring and mouths agape as if arguing over parentage, were the exsanguinated heads of Baldwin and Peck.

Jeff slowly approached the grisly decorations. The blood had pooled and coagulated on the hearthstone. The look of horror on Peck's face mirrored the expression on Jeff's as he slowly reached out to remove it, noting there was only one eye. Where was the other eye?

A sudden noise behind him jerked him around, sending the head flying across the room for the second time within a few hours. It hit the telephone as it rang again, the receiver falling off the hook onto the desk.

"Hello?"

A woman's voice.

"Jeff? Are you there?"

"H'lo?" he said gruffly into the receiver.

"Oh, I'm sorry, Jeff, did I wake you? It's Jennifer."

"No. I was up."

"Ted told me you were up early. We've been up all night."

"Me, too," he said, shoving the head away from him across the desk so that the eye stared out of the window, Under the head, the Yellow Pages of the Phone Directory were opened to the letter 'P'. He hadn't used the book, had he? No, it was always tucked away in the middle drawer of the desk. He only half-heard Jennifer still talking.

"We just haven't seen you since… before…"

"I know."

"Mom is making breakfast for us and we wondered if you wanted to join us. Have something to eat before the funeral?"

Funeral? Did they know? Oh, wait. No. It was Buddy's funeral today.

"I couldn't eat… that is, something has happened. The owner of this place…"

He remembered a motto a friend of his had come up with once: *'Tell the truth when you can…'*

"…died. Suddenly."

"Oh, Jeff, I'm so sorry."

"It's okay. I didn't really know him well. I was just the caretaker, but he's got some people coming over this morning."

As he fabricated, his eyes roved over the page of the phone book. Alistair liked the desk neat, everything put away. His head was messing up the feng shui.

"You'll miss the funeral?"

"Everything happens at once, doesn't it?" he said. He scanned the book before him. Had Alistair used the book? Not while Jeff was in the room… wait. When he went to the barn for the screen.

"They say deaths come in threes."

Jeff's eyes flicked to the lawn and back to the mantel

and he agreed with her. What would he want in the Yellow Pages: plexiglas, plimsolls, plinths, plows…?

"Did they say how long they needed you up there?" Jennifer asked, then called back away from the phone, "No, he can't, Mother. Another death."

Plugs, plumage…

"No, you don't know him," she continued. "Just a minute, let me finish with Jeff."

Jeff moved Alistair's head a bit and there it was underlined:

Plumber.

On the pad under Alistair's left ear, in impeccable Palmer script: 'Sunday. 10:30am'.

No!

A plumber. Coming here. Today. The blocked pipe. The blood… The *bodies*.

"Jennifer, I have to go get ready. I'll try to come by this afternoon, if he's done by then."

"Please do, Jeff, Mother has enough food for an army."

Jeff almost gagged.

"Come anytime."

"I'll try. Maybe early afternoon. I'll have to be back here for tonight." His eye was caught by a sunbeam through the window, illuminating a sheet of paper. "Papers to sign," he added. He reached down and picked up the paper, already signed by the eager dead owner. The deed to the property.

"Okay, Jeff," Jennifer said. "Sorry again for your… loss."

'*Tell the truth when you can,*' he heard the motto in his head, '*but shovel it deep when you must.*'

A plumber. Coming here. This morning... Shovel it deep when you must.

Jeff rolled the bits and pieces up in the hand-woven rug They weighed surprisingly little. So much had been ingested. Not *di*gested, but *in*gested. The rug had been very absorbent. He could cover where the limbs had lain with a small throw rug, also wand-woven by Letitia, depicting the transfer of half of the house down Racebrook Road. By oxen. It was maroon. Perfect. The arterial spray from the double decapitation had mainly splattered across the larger rug. He'd have to do a more intensive clean of the hearthstone and mantel later, but first he would have to make sure none of the remains remained.

He checked his watch.

This town was very quiet on a Sunday. The church traffic on Racebrook wouldn't begin for another couple of hours. He had a lot to do before the plumber arrived.

He dragged the rolled-up rug towards the door where he'd placed a large black Hefty bag, oversized 'for big jobs'. The rug fit halfway into it. He had to pull another down from the top to cover the whole thing. He tightened the plastic ties in the middle and hefted the load up onto his shoulder. Something shifted inside to drop to the end of the bag hanging down his back. Probably a head. Jeff smiled grimly, thinking of Peck and Baldwin together for eternity.

Parts of them, anyway, he thought. The parts that haven't become parts of *me*.

Stepping out onto the porch, he scanned the lawn where he had gorged on Alistair Peck.

"Our blood is this land," Alistair had bragged often enough. "Our blood and sweat."

Jeff was fairly sure Alistair had never sweated in his life, but he could agree with him heartily about the blood. Jeff had saturated the area with the hose, washing off the porch and the walkway, spreading lime from a large bag in the barn onto the area. The plumber would never notice. And he needn't go into the living room to deal with the pipes. Jeff felt fairly safe, but he'd have to work quickly.

First the car.

Then the carcasses.

A short time later, in a large house not far from the Peck homestead, on a street where no insects chirped and no birds sang, a maid approached a butler with trepidation.

"The master's bed hasn't been slept in," she said.

"The Head of the Household's actions are of no concern to you," he replied, austerely.

"Sorry, sir. I only told you because…"

"I am perfectly aware of the situation," he said. "Thank you, Mary. See if Cook needs help in the kitchen."

"Yes, sir. Sorry, sir." Mary turned to make her way downstairs.

"And Mary," the butler said, standing by the front window, looking down the drive.

"Yes, sir?"

He half-turned to her. "No mention below stairs about the sleeping arrangements."

"No, sir. I mean, yes, sir."

"Wait."

Mary stopped again by the green baize door that led to the lower level.

"I see his car. It's just outside the gates. You may let Cook know that Mr Baldwin has returned."

Odd that the car hadn't come *through* the gates. It had stopped by the curb, the front of it just visible past the pillars that flanked the drive. He walked out to see if he could be any assistance to the Head of the Household and found the *head* of the Head of the Household mounted on a spike adorning the ornamental ironwork of the gate.

The graveyard on Racebrook was several hundred feet downhill from the old Peck homestead. Few people came to this place these days, just a caretaker once a month to cut the grass. The area was quite full of the original settlers settling down into the loam. The pit Jeff dug wasn't the proper length or depth. There was little left of these two bodies to decay or attract animals. He tossed the Hefty bag containing the bits and bones wrapped up in the rug into the hole. Two bodies, one head.

Alistair had planned so much in advance. When he had buried his Mother here, he had the stone carved with her name in the centre. Below and to the left, *his* name had already been carved with his birth date and a dash. He had always been so worried about having enough money to cover his final years. Jeff saw to it that Alistair didn't even have to pay for his funeral.

Jeff emptied the bag of lime over the Hefty bag and filled in the grave. He threw some grass seed over the newly-dug earth and then covered the area with leaves. By the time the groundskeeper came by the trim the weeds, there would be a covering of grass on the grave. Shouldering the shovel, Jeff started back toward the house. If the plumber was on time, he might even be able to make it to Buddy's service.

Buddy.

He stood there right in front of Jeff at the entrance to the cemetery. His lips were moving but Jeff could hear no sound. Jeff could see every detail in Buddy's face, every wrinkle in his clothing, but he could still see *through* him. Buddy pointed at Jeff with an urgency Jeff felt in his soul and… a truck drove up over the hill, rattling past the gate. On the side of the truck was painted, 'Pete's Plumbing. We're 'Plumb' Good!'

When Jeff glanced back from the road, Buddy was gone. Jeff took off at a loping run for the house.

"I got here a little early," Pete said, unpacking his toolkit from behind the front seat of his truck. "Figured, start early, finish early."

Jeff grunted. He noticed he was barely winded from his short jog up the road, Although seemingly out of shape, his stamina, especially over the course of the three nights of the fullest moon had marvellously increased.

"I guess you have one of these?" Pete pulled out a plunger.

"Don't know," Jeff said. "Maybe."

"Sometimes that's all you need," Pete said. "But I don't mind coming out on a day off. What else do I have to do? Besides, I've helped the Pecks out for some time now. Hear they're maybe sellin' the place?"

"He talked about it," Jeff said, leaning the shovel against the side of the porch.

"A shame. Been in the family for centuries." Pete stepped up onto the porch. 'It's a strange house, though. Only one toilet and all the way down at this end. If you have to get up in the night, it's a long trek. Sink's in the hall outside the bathroom. If they were adding on a room to put plumbing in, you'd think they would have made it big enough to hold all the plumbing, wouldn't you think?"

Jeff gestured that Pete should go on ahead of him into the house.

Pete continued talking. "Well, let's see what's going on. Hopefully nothing too serious. You doing some work around the house?"

"Some reseeding," Jeff gestured with a thumb over

his shoulder. "And re-varnishing the floors in the living room."

"Uh huh. Is he around today? Mr Peck?"

"No," Jeff said, standing beside the sink in the hall next to the bathroom.

"No? Saw his car in the upper drive. Just wondered."

Jeff glanced toward the barn. "He… had a funeral to go to." (*Tell the truth when you must…*)

"Oh. Shame." Pete plunged some more. The water stayed the same level in the bowl. "Someone he was close to?"

"Yeah. Do you know about how long this will take? I have a service to make as well, if I can."

"Seems to be a clog down there. I'll get the snake. Shouldn't take too long, but these old pipes…" Pete walked back up to his truck, hiking up his pants as he went.

Jeff gave a quick scan of the small bathroom. Nothing evident, no blood he could see. He grabbed a Kleenex and swiped it over the shower drain, clearing away some hair that had gathered there. Then, on instinct, he flushed the toilet. And the water began to fill the bowl quickly rather than empty it. Jeff lunged for the valve under it, managing to turn off the water right at the rim.

"Now, you just let me see to this," Pete said, appearing in the doorway with his plumber's snake. "Sometimes help is more of a hindrance."

Jeff said, "I'll just go inside." He stopped, filling the doorway with his bulk. "If you… need anything, call out. Don't come in. The floors…"

"That's fine, that's fine. I've got everything I need out here." Pete set to work, carefully inserting the snake down inside the bowl, careful to keep the plastic sleeve over the coil so as not to scratch the porcelain.

"What a day," Jeff muttered, closing the living room door behind him. "What a day, what a day, whataday!" His eyes darted from floor to mantel to rug to desk. "What else, what else, what else, what else…"

He went into the small kitchen, managed with difficulty to pull a rubber pan out from under the sink, and poured bleach into it, then some Pine-sol, then filled the pan with cold water. Cold for blood, right? He seemed to remember that from somewhere. Cold for blood. Finding an old sponge under the sink as well, he threw that into the liquid, pulled on a pair of rubber gloves and got to work on the mantel. This cleaning wouldn't stand up to a forensics inspection, but if there was no suspicion of foul play, this room wouldn't be subjected to an inspection anyway. He started to scrub the hearthstones.

The head.

Why had he left the head?!

As a warning. "*Stay away from me.*" So there *would* be an investigation. Who killed Mr Baldwin? Did anyone know he was coming here? Jeff scrubbed harder. If they did know and came here to question him, the final night of the full moon would give them the answer. But only if they came tonight. He had to get away for the day. He would go to Buddy's service once the plumber was gone. He threw the dirty water into the kitchen sink and then scrubbed the graveyard dirt from under his fingernails. He shouldn't have left the head. Everyone could have assumed Baldwin had run off somewhere. The desk! I have to clean off the desk!

"How's it going?" Jeff asked, stepping down the one step into the hall, while closing the door behind him.

"Something's down there alright," Pete said, pausing to wipe the sweat from his forehead with a handkerchief. "I'm windin' er back up now. I think I've got it." He wiggled the handle again and slowly started to retract the coil. "So many things can mess up these old pipes. Could be just mineral deposits, could be something accidentally flushed?"

Jeff shrugged.

"Could even be tree roots. Those are particularly tough to fix. It feels like it's moving, though. Just comin' around the U-bend now. Here it comes."

A discoloured mass caught for a moment, broke free and floated up into the bowl. Caught in the coil was a twig-like object.

"Looks like roots… nope… what *is* that?" Pete knelt down, peering into the bowl. "Did you try to flush some… bones?"

The mass that floated up was rather shaped like an oval with maybe roots attached to the back of it.

"Well, here it comes, whatever it is," Pete muttered. "Didn't take too long, after all. Now we'll see…"

The oval shape rotated in the water.

A human eye looked up out of the bowl at Pete. Pete skittered backwards, falling on his backside. He looked quickly up at Jeff, but Jeff was already looking at *him*.

🦆

Jeff finished smoothing the soil in the basement so that it was flat. He had always thought it odd to see a basement that had never been finished off, just a house built on dirt, the foundation rocks piled up like a stone wall. No mortar. Odd, but convenient. As he worked, his thoughts drifted. "Put up." Why is it when you make preserves you "put them up" and then store them down in the cellar? Why is it when you kill something, you "put them down" and sometimes, not usually but sometimes, put them in the cellar as well? The English language was fascinating.

He found himself humming a song, an old drinking song from college as he dragged some musty old crates over the spot…

> "And he that will this health deny,
> Down among the dead men,
> Down among the dead men,
> Down, down, down, down,
> Down among the dead men let him lie."

Lumbering upstairs, he turned off the light. Once again, he stripped off and showered. A lot of deaths this weekend. He knew he wouldn't make it to Buddy's funeral. He'd already been to two today. Should the first one count as two? Maybe. He'd been to three today. This last one had numbed him. He had never knowingly killed someone before and he felt vaguely removed from it. But the toilet was fixed.

He dried himself off on the way up to his bedroom, dropping the towel over the doorknob as he entered. What to wear, what to wear? Or more accurately, what would fit, what would fit?

But he would go to the Hamilton's house. He knew what he had to do next. It was very clear to him and he had to do it today. That bicycle. All of this came down to that bicycle. He knew where it was and that it had been repaired and was waiting for the next one of them to ride it. That was the cause of everything. He had been riding it when he was attacked and infected with this curse, Sam had been riding it the year before when he disappeared, Buddy had been riding it…

None of this would have happened if it weren't for that bike.

And Jeff was going to destroy it before it hurt anyone else.

R. Bruce Connelly is a professional actor, director and Muppet who lives in New York City. This is the seventh episode in his 'Bike Cycle' series of stories. The previous ones can be read in Harvey Duckman Presents, Vols. 1-4, 6 and 7.

When Harvey called and asked if the 'Bike Cycle' had a Plumbing Story to include in their Plumbing Special, I said, "Well, there is one but I don't know if you will want me to write it."

But he did want me to.

So I did.

Not my fault.

Now that you've read it, I can only add, "Are you alright?"

SUPER BARRIO MOTHERS

WILL NETT

"What happens is, when these pipe joints are moulded, they get rough edges... like that, look. 'Ere, feel that."

The plumber ran two fingers around the inside edge of the pipe he had just detached.

I was not paying attention. He was the spitting image of Richard Harris.

Plumbledore.

"They should be chamfered off before they're fitted, otherwise long hair gets snagged on 'em, and that's how they get blocked up."

He disappeared beneath the kitchen cupboards, again, on his back. His voice grew muffled.

"You better tell your old lady to be more careful in future. When she gets in."

My old lady?

"I don't live here, mate," I said. "I'm just staying for a few days."

"Where you from?" he shouted.

"Boro," I said.

He did not reply.

"Or tell her to get her haircut," he said, after a short silence.

"It's three lads who live here," I explained, "and one of em's as bald as a fucking egg."

"Well, they must be doing alright with the Jack and Danny, then," he said, throwing another fistful of long matted hair onto the kitchen floor.

"We're in Shoreditch," I said, "the sewers'll be carpeted in hipsters' beard hair."

He slid out from beneath the cupboard, his long grey hair billowing out like steam at the sides.

"£150, mate, anyway," he said casually, reaching for his teacup.

My phone rang, almost instantaneously.

It was my mate, Chris. "Can you pay the plumber when he's finished? I'll sort you out later. Should be about £70."

My hand was already in my pocket.

"Fucking London," I sighed, counting out five £20 notes. "Stand around in someone's kitchen for ten minutes and you're on the hook for a £150."

"Typical Yorkshireman," the plumber said. "I haven't charged you for the tea, have I?" as he folded the notes into the pocket of his boiler suit. "Anyway, you're lucky I could get here at such short notice. It's a war zone, this plumbing racket these days."

"So, I've heard," I said.

Since the Thames Barrier was overwhelmed by the Great Rising of 2022, which, along with the Barrier itself, had submerged most of the surrounding area, a turf war involving the big water companies of the 2020s had spread throughout the former capital.

From Southend, all the way east as far as Isle of Dogs belonged to the North Sea. London City Airport, the O2 Arena, and the southern end of the Blackwall Tunnel were lost to the flooding. Only at Rotherhithe, and the higher ground of Stave Hill Eco Park, did the southern half of the city begin to reappear.

As ever, the government kept their feet dry, having moved the Treasury, and Parliament, to Darlington in the north.

The internecine plumbing wars were violent as an entire subterranean community took refuge in the surrounding sewers of Lewisham, Peckham and Battersea. The population of the city was almost halved as the flooding continued throughout the winter of 2022/2023. Much of North London had survived, but had become overrun by the exodus of refugees from the South. The ongoing gentrification that had seized Hackney, Dalton, and Stoke Newington, to name but three areas north of the Thames, was undone in a matter of months as thousands of families descended upon its sewers, subways and streets.

The Prime Minister's typically blustering announcement in the days afterwards, that "we MUST stay afloat. We WILL stay afloat" had gone down in history as one of his more absurd pronouncements when it was discovered that the government had ignored warnings from as early as 2012 that the Barrier would require considerable enforcement work in order to combat the threat of Global Warming.

Now, in 2050, with that particular Prime Minister currently carrying the unwanted historical first of being imprisoned, Swedish Prime Minister Greta Thunberg, the one-time child-sized thorn in the side of global governments, leads the clean-up operation for Europe.

The pre-flood plumbing companies, like the society that they now served, in the south of the country at least, had splintered off into tribal groups akin to those of medieval Britain. They were formed through a kinship born out of likewise nationalities, sexualities, or ages, amongst other things. There were the French engineering students that made up Le Plomb Squad, and the Silverfish, a creaking band of over 60s that comprised the plumber from Chris's house. It was Plumbledore who first brought this underground war to my attention.

The Mad Men, named for a play on words of the Arabic term for 'tidal', 'el Mad' were drawn from local Arab communities.

The Bleeders and the Macerators, as you might expect from those names, were at war amongst themselves, having previously been the collective known as Flange 22. They were considered to be the most violent of these new battalions and their time was spent less manipulating the water supply, than engaged in violent pitched battles.

Slough Sludge, plc. shored up the ever wet westlands, and the Floozies flew the flag for feminism.

The overall rulers of this new hierarchy of the

waterways were the Super Barrio Mothers, Rosalina and Ana Martinez, Basque sisters with a 'land crew' of over three hundred 'rompiente' and equal number in subterranean 'fontaneros'.

Above ground, all across what remained of 'dry' London, the 'rompiente' ran riot, as the name suggests, sabotaging the work of rival firms, in an unstoppable crimewave of violence, murder, corporate vandalism and general larceny. Operating alongside them, or beneath, were the actual plumbers, effectively engaged in a racket whereby they controlled much of the capital's water flow.

"On and off, like a tap," became their unofficial motto, often repeated to various civic leaders and rivals, usually as the subject was choked out with a length of piping across the throat, or a rubber-soled boot pressed against the cheek.

They were out of control, and at the same time, almost entirely in control of the water supply across six hundred square miles.

I've never seen an office like Rosalina Martinez's before. It was accessed via the old Wapping Hydraulic Power Station, beside Shadwell Basin. The Basin itself was now a marine depot for the might of the Super Barrio Mothers' machinery and fleet, and throbbed with activity not seen in the area since the Industrial Revolution. The Maynard Quay was effectively a workshop, given over to breakers and engineers clattering away at anything from decommissioned yachts to customised jet skis. Wapping

Woods to the east had been flattened to give land access to vehicles via Garnet Street. The whole area was cordoned off and heavily guarded, to the North alongside the A1203, The Highway, and to the east at the Wapping Wall and Thames Path.

A custom-built diesel silo loomed high over the Peartree Lane area, the fumes fogging the air. The guards, who wore customary red headgear of all types, bandanas, baseball caps, bike helmets, had the typically heavy-handed demeanour of untrained militia groups that had been bestowed with weapons and authority.

A pair of them shunted me from the Garnet Street gates to the old pumping house with little ceremony, and ushered me into the precarious-looking hydraulic lift that took me a hundred and fifty feet beneath the streets of London. The expected miasma of raw sewage hovered in the air as we plunged past various levels of activity. Air vents and steam pipes belched sporadically as the temperature began to rise when we neared the bottom.

One of the guards shunted the huge car doors open and bade me straight ahead. It was the only direction we could go in. Behind was nothing but solid brick wall. The arched ceiling released an occasional drip of moisture as we approached an enormous vault door. The 'handle' was a polished brass wheel, about the size of a car steering wheel, and nothing of its appearance suggested what was about to be revealed behind it.

One of the guards firmly spun the wheel and the door

clanked open. He drew it back to a channel of brilliant white light that flooded the outer corridor.

I winced at the light that rushed into my eyes.

"Welcome to my Alhambra," said a voice, as clear and sharp as Lalique glass.

As the door was closed shut behind me by the guard, my eyes were able to focus, but were no less dazzled, this time by the mosaic floor that stretched away to Rosa Martinez's desk, from where the greeting had carried. Every inch of the room was struck from floor to ceiling with tilework that even a layman such as myself understood was impressive.

"Timurid, Mocarabe, Delft…it's all here. Azulejo is, of course, my favourite," Rosa said, fluttering a hand.

The room was cavernous, its ceiling arched and adorned in the Muqarna style that gave rise to the Mocarabe that Rosa had highlighted.

She interrupted as I tried to rein in my gawping.

"Call it a 'stew'," she said, "or, as I prefer, 'bangio'."

Millennia of history surrounded us. More, even. Furnishings and sanitation. Artistic brilliance. Craftsmanship unequalled in the modern day.

"A drink, Mr Nett?" she asked, summoning a servant I had not even noticed. He shuffled towards us in bare feet, his hands crossed at his stomach.

"I'll have a gin and tonic," I said, "and take it easy with the tonic."

He faded away quietly amongst the Doric columns, an

open bathing area replete with fountains and steam baths. It was a veritable hammam, screened off for the most part by silk curtains.

"You take your drink strong, Mr Nett," she said. "I am hearing this about writers."

"I take it any way I can get it when I'm sitting in a palatial bathhouse somewhere at the bottom of the Thames," I said.

"After the Flood, some of us floated to the top, others drowned," she explained.

Her skin was as white as the bone china teapot that was returned on a silver tray by the servant, alongside my drink. He placed the tray on the green marbled desk between us as I sat down. Any semblance of Hispanic skin tones were long gone. These were dark times, above and below ground. No sunlight at this depth. Her flaxen hair was shaved to above her bejewelled ears, in a style we knew at the turn of the century as a 'step'.

"I keep my hair short," she explained, "all over my body."

She waited for a reaction, but none came.

"To save water, you understand," she added, making a hair washing motion with her hands.

She studied me the way a cat does its own reflection in a mirror, as her eyes flashed the same shade of blue as the Delft tiling.

"The name is unofficial," she started, pouring her tea. Her fingers were long, her nails painted in the Spanish colours. "I know you pressmen, or whatever you are now, like the video game connection. You go back to the Dry and your Editor prints some 'mierda' next to some pictures."

The Dry was the name for what little was left of any parts of the city that were unflooded.

"You, and your sister, are probably the most powerful women, people, in the southern half of England. Fuck it, the whole country."

I'd relaxed somewhat, and slipped out of my usual professional journalistic vernacular. I suspected that she had that effect on most men.

"That may be so," she replied, "but in wartime, balances are easily tipped."

"And what of Ana?" I pressed.

"Ah, now we get to business. Is she married? Is she single? Blah, blah, blah. Typical English paper talk. I thought those days were gone."

I gazed at the ceramic bas-relief of the Martinez family that took up much of the wall space behind Rosa's head. I always found such art to be tacky and self-indulgent, but, as with its surrounds, this was an undeniably impressive work. Rosa, her father Goncalvo, the 'Grand Old Man of the Waterworks' as he was often referred to in the press, Senora Martina, the classic Iberian matriarch, and the rarely seen Ana.

"Ana is more, how do you say…? 'Hands-on'," Rosa said, confirming diplomatically what I already knew, that this Spanish furie ran the street level operations that held the city in its grip. "I am the, shall we say, 'respectable face' of London's water provisions, now."

"And the 'End Game'…" I said, "is there one?"

"This is a backwards country, Mr Nett," she said. "The Romans were here for around four hundred years, and introduced to these lands technologies that were unimaginable. So, unimaginable, in fact, that when the Romans left, the locals reverted to shitting off bridges into the Thames for the next thousand years, and more. I don't see anyone with the power to 'Take Back Control'."

I grinned, in agreement, more than anything else.

She laughed out loud.

"What is this obsession with slogans in this country? You fall for it… everytime. My favourite is 'Control The Borders'. Always three words with these people. My father would say 'but they could not even control the Thames Barrier when they were at the controls'."

I glanced around the room, my mind agreeing with her. This far down I expected the stench of raw sewage, but everything was controlled. The temperature was above average, certainly, presumably as you would expect at that depth. The room smelt of rosewater, and jasmine.

Occasionally, a worker would appear, engaged contentedly in some sanitary endeavour, the decanting of water, preservation of the tilework or scientific experiment. It all went on in the area to the right of where we were sitting.

Opposite was a relaxation suite of sorts, floatation tanks, bathing pools and the like. None were occupied.

"Governments don't like us because holding the country to ransom is traditionally their business. Now it belongs to the people. I can speak to the Prime Minister within minutes, and if she upsets me, she'll be without bathwater within twenty four hours."

"That's quite a claim," I said, making a note in my pad. I could already see my Editor salivating over it as it was laid out for tomorrow's copy.

She leaned forward in her chair and fixed me with a half-smiling stare. "I'm divorced twice," she said. "I know all about squeezing a man's cojones until his supply is cut off."

I wrote that quote down in capitals, imagining it would leapfrog the previous one.

"It will be the way of all utilities, probably in our lifetime. The Mars landings have not returned a single drop of water. The Venus Project is still at least two years away from take off. Electricity, fresh air, what's left of it, that is, will all be returned to the people. It is already happening It has always been said that the seas will reclaim the land, and we see that now. I am surprised it has taken this long."

"Will the Human Race survive?" I asked.

"It must learn to swim," she said, "and fast."

Middlesbrough author Will Nett's global appeal and general popularity have seen his writing career straddle two Millennia. His work has appeared across a wide range of publications, from his ever-popular books, to short-form contributions for institutions such as Crossing The Tees, and Arts Council England. He is an incurable backpacker, amateur musician, and habitual note-maker/taker, most of which have found their way into his Gonzo-steeped books, My Only Boro: A Walk Through Red & White, his riotous travelogue, Billy No Maps: Teessider On Tour, Local Author Writes Book, and The Golfer's Lament. His anthology, Bank Notes, collecting together his strange tales in the vein of the work included here was released in 2021. Find Will on Twitter @will_nett

THE FLATMATE

DAVID SACKS

Well, here we are; this is my new flat. I just moved in about a week ago. I wasn't planning on moving to a new place so soon, but my previous flatmate turned out to be a bit of a drag. So, I've relocated. Come on, let me show you around.

Over there, sitting at the desk, working on his computer, is my new flatmate, Harold. He's a quiet sort and we don't really interact. Harold's bedroom is over there. And across the hall, is my room. I also have kitchen privileges, but I generally try not to get in his way when he's cooking. He seems to have a bit of a temper when he's cooking. I've offered to help with the dishes, but he clearly prefers to do things himself. I think he might be a little bit of a control freak, but that's okay; I can deal with it.

Sometimes he has a friend spend the night. Her name is Claire. She's not any more sociable than he is, but that's okay. I usually just stay in my room when she's here. I don't bother her, and she doesn't bother me.

The last place I lived wasn't very far from here. It was a little nicer, though. The appliances were more high-end, and the fixtures in the kitchen and bathroom were more modern. But, I'm just happy to have a roof over my head and not have to spend any more nights on the street. You don't really know how much it means to have a place to live until you've lived on the street. People just walk right over you as if you're not even there. Or, if they're really mean, or drunk, sometimes they'll even try to step on you. You have to be alert every single minute; you can't let your guard down for even a fraction of a second! Not only that, but when you live on the street, you always have to scrounge for food. And there's so much competition. Everyone and everything out there is scavenging for food.

So, I'm going to try really hard not to mess this up. I'm going to be respectful of Harold's space and just keep to myself. No matter how good his dinner smells, I'm not going to try to sneak a taste. No matter how cold it gets at night, I'm not going to try to crawl into bed with him. I think that crawling into bed on a cold night thing is what got me kicked out of my previous flat. Honestly, though, Marvin was fast asleep; I didn't think he'd even notice I was there. But, alas, he woke up, threw me up against the wall and when I came to, everything was spinning.

Marvin was a real hypocrite, you know? I mean, sometimes he'd come into my room at night, and I never got all bent out of shape about it… as long as he didn't march in in the middle of the night unannounced and turn on the light. Once he came into my room at about 3am and turned on the light and I nearly had a heart attack. He, who had room-darkening shades on his bedroom windows, thinks nothing of barging into my room and flicking on the light? How freaking bizarre is that? And how inconsiderate! Now that I think about it, Marvin was a real jerk!

So, even though Harold is a little standoffish, I think maybe he's going to be easier to live with than Marvin was. I think maybe getting evicted from my previous flat wasn't such a bad thing after all. I think maybe things really do happen for the best.

Uh-oh. Maybe I spoke too soon. Harold, it seems, is quite highly strung and is currently going ballistic because it appears that the toilet has become blocked. He's pacing back and forth and yelling into the phone that a plumber needs to come immediately and unblock it. He has called a number of plumbers and, so far, none of them can get here quickly enough to please Harold, and he's becoming absolutely frantic because Claire is due to arrive any minute.

Ah! He's finally reached someone who can come straight away, but instead of being relieved and calming down, now he's ranting that it's going to cost him at least £112. I guess I should just be thankful that he doesn't think

I had anything to do with the toilet becoming blocked. However, rather than push my luck, I think I'll just stay out of sight until this is resolved.

Well, now Claire has arrived, and of course, she wants to use the loo. Harold is absolutely mortified. He apologises profoundly and explains that the loo is inoperative at the moment.

"But the plumber is on the way," he assures her. "He'll be here any minute."

"I only want to freshen up a bit," she says.

But before they can discuss it any further, the plumber arrives. He strides in and kneels down next to the toilet.

"What seems to be the issue?" he asks.

"It's blocked," Harold says.

"Okay, let's have a look at it," says the plumber.

Harold, Claire, and I all stand around and watch the plumber have a look at the loo. After a moment or two, he reaches into his bag and pulls out a drain snake.

"You might want to stand back," he tells us.

We all take a step back. It's rather tight in there, so one step back is about all we can take.

The plumber goes to work and in a few short minutes, he reels in the snake and removes it.

"Would you look at that!" he says.

"What is it?" asks Harold.

"Voila," says the plumber, holding up a rather large earring, "Here's your blockage!"

And then to Claire, "It appears you've misplaced an earring, Madame."

Claire stares at the earring, dumbfounded.

"How did you drop an earring in the loo?" Harold asks her.

Claire still appears confused.

"That's not my earring," she says.

"Well, then, whose is it?" asks Harold, who immediately wishes he hadn't because, now, Claire is wondering the same thing.

"That's a damn good question, Harold! Whose bloody earring is it?"

"Don't look at me!" says the plumber.

"Whose bloody earring is it, Harold!" she repeats, giving him a shove for good measure.

Harold is stammering and stuttering. Frankly, I've never seen him quite so undone.

"I don't know! I don't know whose earring it is!" he squeaks. "I swear, I'm not seeing anyone else! I don't know where the earring came from!"

I know it's never good to get involved when two lovers are having an argument.

"Do not engage… do not engage… do not engage… do not engage…" I repeat to myself, in order to keep myself from, well, engaging. That's always been my motto and I silently chant it like a mantra when I'm tempted to insert myself where I don't belong.

But all that drama is starting to get on my nerves, and

I can see it's starting to get on the plumber's nerves as well.

"Stop yelling!" I yell, jumping in front of them, "I know you love each other, so just stop yelling! Maybe the earring has been in there for years and has just now moved to a spot that caused it to become stuck! Or maybe it came down through the drainpipe from the flat upstairs! It's not her earring; it's not your earring; it's not my earring; it's not the plumber's earring. Just pay the man his £112 and we can all get on with our day!"

"£175," says the plumber.

"£175??" shrieks Harold.

"You said it was an emergency; emergency calls are £175," the plumber says with a shrug.

Now, out of the blue, Claire is screaming. It's sort of a cross between a scream of terror and a scream of disgust.

"Now what?" says Harold, nearing the end of his tether.

"A cockroach!" she screeches.

"Ewww!" I say. "A cockroach? Where?"

She thrusts out her quivering arm and points. Everyone turns and looks to where she's pointing.

What the…? Why is she pointing at me?

"Whoa! That's a big son of a gun!" says the plumber.

Harold, obviously not in his right mind, lunges and

tries to stomp on me, but my reflexes are pretty good and I manage to dodge him. Claire continues to scream and point and dance about. I don't really like to fly, but I will when I have to. I take off and Harold starts swatting at me, but he's so freaked out by everything that's happening, he's just swinging wildly. I'm almost to the door when one of his wild swings catches me and slams me into the wall. I'm stunned, truly stunned.

As I lie, dazed, on the cold tile, I'm somewhat aware of the plumber lifting me up by one of my antennae and dropping me into the crapper. Then everything starts spinning.

Well, here we are; this is my new flat. I've been relocated again. Come on, let me show you around. Over there, sitting in front of the telly, eating crisps and dip, is my new flatmate, Amanda.

Mmmm… I love crisps. They're my favourite. I simply can't resist them. I wonder if, maybe, she might drop me a crumb or two…

Davia Sacks is a professional actor, singer and writer, residing in New York City. She has performed on Broadway, National Tours, Regional Theatre, and a number of jazz and pop albums. An alumnus of the Tony-honoured BMI Musical Theatre Workshop, she was one of twenty composer-lyricists chosen to be published in the BMI Musical Theatre Songbook.

Her short story, The Curse of Beauty, was included in Harvey Duckman Presents Volume 8, and she is delighted and honoured to be included in Volume 9!

Her current projects include two full-length plays, a collection of short plays and monologues, a novella, and of course, more short stories.

THE RAT IN THE DRAIN

PETER JAMES MARTIN

I've been in stranger circumstances, that much is true. I was chased by garden gnomes once. Another time I had to help train a young banshee. However, there is still something genuinely odd about trying to talk to someone by yelling down a drain pipe.

"Riz, if you can, you need to go for the left exit, the left exit!"

"Bren, I dunno how many times I can tell yer dis, but dere is no soddin left exit! If yer gunna giv me directions, start givin me ones I can fukin use!"

You try to help someone, and this is the thanks you get. No surprises to say that the only reason that Riz was in this network of plumbing was because we were helping someone out. It had all started a few hours ago.

We were in my office, bemoaning the lack of jobs currently on offer for us.

"Here's one… Thomas Maverick?" I said, tapping away on my phone.

"Can't, pissed in his shoes, member," Riz moaned as he tossed another paper ball into the bin.

"Right, I'll add his name to the list of clients who'll probably put a hit out on us sooner or later. If there's space that is." I offered another suggestion. "What about this job then? Fern wants a pair of hands to help with overgrown Mandrakes?"

Riz just looked at me, and I rolled my eyes.

"Yeah, okay, not a good idea after last time." I moved on from that one as well. "We need to find something we can do! Alice is expecting money off us!" I pointed out, hoping it might stir Riz into some sort of action.

"If she wants der cash dat bad, she can bloody find us a job ta pay fer it! Othawise she can sod off!" Riz rolled over onto his back, his little podgy rat belly swaying with the motion. My phone going off quickly jolted him onto all fours:

"Bloody eck! She musta be listenin in ta us! Throw der phone out da window! Quick!"

"I'm not throwing my phone out of the window! It's not even Alice!"

"Well, if it's not Alice, den who der heck is it!" Riz asked a very good question.

"Let me find out then!" I yelled at him, before checking to see that I hadn't already answered it, meaning that I just shouted at whoever was on the other end. Wouldn't be a great way to start any conversation.

"Hello?" I asked with some trepidation.

"Is that Brennan? The guy with the weird talking rat?"

Well, whoever it was hadn't insulted me or Riz, so we were off to a good start.

"That would be me. Who may I say is asking?"

A question that could have dangerous results depending on what they said. Already I had the following information about the caller. He was a man, sounding middle aged. Not a lot to go on, you'd agree. As it turned out, who the caller actually was, I'd never have guessed in a billion years. More or less.

"Don't you remember me? It's me, Karl Acton, the plumber who helped you find that Rune thingy?"

That was another event that I had consciously submerged into the darkest parts of my memory. To put it simply, Riz had been trying to show me a Rune he'd crafted that would supposedly turn a pile of ingredients into a parmo. Yes, he was still drunk at the time. No, it didn't work. The Rune failed to do anything, and Riz being drunk Riz, threw it down the drain, because he's a smegging idiot. This was when the Rune did choose to activate, of course and flooded the drainage with a magical substance that I can only dub, sploop. You can use the word if you want to.

To clear this, we had to bring in a plumber, and through the event, where the sploop gained some kind of sentience, I really can't explain that part, the plumber became aware of Riz and all that came with that. A fantastic day's work there, I think you'll agree.

Anyway, as a result of that, we said that if Karl ever got into a problem like that, he could call us to take care of it. This was the day he called us in.

"Yes, I remember you, Karl. You promised not to sue

us over the sploop thing. Please don't tell me there's more of that," I semi-pleaded down the phone.

"Oh god, no. This one is more, tentacley?"

There's an adjective you never want to hear, tentacley. It's right up there with slimey, gooey and murdery.

"You want us in on this job?" I asked, already knowing the response.

"I wouldn't have rang up otherwise! It's a place in Fairfield, big house, bad plumbing. I'll text you the address. If you could get here quickly, that would be grand!" Karl said, before hanging up.

"Do yer think he'll giv us a cut of der cash?" Riz asked, somewhat hopefully.

"Depends on if we screw the job up, doesn't it," I said as I pulled myself out of the chair, stretching as if I had spent the last four hours sitting there. I knew it wasn't, it was closer to six.

Just as Karl had promised, he texted me the details and within quarter of an hour, we pulled up outside a property in Fairfield. It looked like a conversion of some sort but what the old building had been wasn't clear. A beaten and worn For Sale sign hinted at what the owner was trying to do, but we'd have to wait and see if there was a connection with them selling and what was going on here. Not that we knew what exactly was going on here ourselves other than a tentacle problem.

The front door was ajar so I didn't bother knocking. On entering, I saw that the hallway, long and narrow, leading to a grand staircase, was a shade of white that made me think of a dentist rather than someone's home. There was no splash of colour at all anywhere. I heard a curious clanging sound though, one at first, I thought was coming from Karl, who must have been at the source of the problem.

"Hello?" I shouted.

Riz was peering around as we went down the hallway, the banging sound strangely keeping up with us, not sounding any further or closer.

"Maybe we shud check dese rooms, yer know, cud be stuff inside ta steal, I mean, der plumber," Riz suggested, and like always, I ignored it. Besides, most of the doors were open, and a peek through revealed nothing but an empty room, all in this irritating white.

I had almost scoured the ground floor when I heard a voice calling me.

"Is that you, Brennan? Did you bring the rat? We need him!" It was definitely Karl, but his voice sounded muffled, like if someone was yelling you a door or two away. I stopped and tried to pinpoint the source. Then I quickly gave up and asked Riz to do it instead since he had the better hearing.

"It's coming from dat way! From behind der stairs."

I followed the way he was pointing but it just led to a painting, oddly put I might add.

It was a very crappy painting, like someone had let a five year old loose with a paintbrush.

"Dat guy's voice is comin from behind ere. Clearly dis is a secret door," Riz then realised what he said and face palmed. "Whoevar built dis place waz an ejit! I mean, come on! A secret door behind der fukin paintin? Who der ell does dat?"

The moron who built this place clearly. Whilst wishing it wasn't true, I felt around the painting and felt a catch. I pressed it and it swung open. The stairway that went down looked nothing like the pristine and bleached décor above. I was glad of the change in scenery. This path was hodgepodge, showing the different building materials that had gone into making it. The clunking and banging I heard was louder down here, and you could hear the ting of metal.

Following a short path to a large room, I saw the broad form of Karl, pushing a bit of wood against something. This 'something' looked like an old boiler but scaled up, a network of pipes emerging from it and spreading out around the house, crossing over with each other seemingly endlessly.

"There you are, mate! Good timing! Didn't think I could hold this bit of wood much more!" He relaxed for just a moment and I saw the tentacle pushing against the wooden plank, dripping ichor. Karl spotted it and whacked it with a nearby hammer.

"Back! Back!" he shouted.

"What the hell is going on here?" I asked, half serious at wanting the question answered.

"Long story short, I was hired to sort the plumbing out, found a monster in it, called you guys!" Karl explained, the fastest I'd ever heard anyone talk. He moved his foot, revealing another pipe jutting out, though there didn't appear to be any appendage sticking out of it at the moment. Didn't mean there wasn't a foul smell coming from it, mind.

"What you waiting for? Stick the rat in!" Karl said, prompting me to take a step back.

"Pardon?" I said, the word slipping out of my mouth.

"Pardon? Dat's all yer got ta fukin say bout dis yer flippin prick! How's bout no, I'm not stickin my trusted business partner in dere! Or, tellin im ta go do one!" Riz yelled, as he crawled out of my pocket.

"Well, I don't know what this even is! I thought you might and you'd fit in the pipe to get it!"

"Like ell I am! Y don't yer do yer soddin job, nd track wat evar it is to its source nd remove it!" Riz wagged his finger at Karl.

"I can split the money with you!"

Those where the magic words Riz had been longing to hear.

"Alrite, I take seventy percent of der cash, yer can keep thirty."

I had been listening to Riz's idea of negotiation, and noticed the big flaw in it straight away.

"Ahem," I coughed to get his attention. "You mean our cash, right?"

"Fine! Fine! Thirty ta me, five ta Bren nd twenty five ta yerself," he offered Karl, thinking that was going to solve my issues. It didn't. Not in the slightest. I was going to start a futile exchange, arguing with him on how these things work, but I saw that Karl's legs were already bending to the strength of the creature pushing forward. Any longer and Karl would be flattened and we would all be in for a bad time.

"Right, we can sort payment out after we sort this creature out!"

"I wanna know how much I'm chargin fer ma dignity ta be crawlin thru a dank pipe!"

With Riz pushing my patience, I knew exactly what I needed to do.

He noticed me behind him. I saw my reflection in his beady little eyes. I also saw the realisation about what I was in the process of doing.

"Bren, can't we talk bout dis first?"

I didn't answer, I was too busy stuffing him head first into the pipe, knowing this was the only way to get this job moving forward. I certainly didn't want to be still here if that creature made it out of the pipes, and I'd like to think the world would have agreed with me. Then again, I knew that everyone that would have met Riz would agree with me shoving him into the pipe, regardless of cause. Hell, some would have gladly paid me to shove him in there. Believe me, I've had offers.

"Yer do dis nd I swear ta all der gods yer world produced dat I'm gunna bite yer nd not let go till I've ripped yer frickin skin off!"

How Riz thought an argument like that would sway me is beyond thinking, and I shoved him head first into the pipe.

"Look at it this way, faster you find the creature, the faster you get to come out of the pipe!" I said. I wasn't expecting a reply, and I wasn't surprised when he didn't. No, what did surprise me was the tentacle that burst out from one of the other pipes, the tentacle that opened out in a hideously toothed maw that was groping about in the darkness. Which might have been fine if I hadn't been occupying the space already.

Riz heard my grunts as I tried to avoid becoming a tasty snack.

"Ha! Who's laughin now smartass! Enjoy becomin food!"

The little prick started laughing but that was cut short when he must have encountered something within the pipes as he started making similar sounds to me.

"Watch out, mate!" Karl said, swinging his hammer round, the blow connecting with the tentacle that was trying to eat me, knocking some of its teeth out with a splash of what I assumed was its blood. The tentacle retreated, and the plumber passed me a plank of wood to cover that particular pipe off with.

"Thanks! Hopefully now Riz can deal with the source of this problem! Any sign of, well, anything?" I asked down the pipe. I heard Riz mutter a few choice words that I presumed were curses aimed at me. "Without, swearing this time!"

"I sed nuthin yet yer treacherous bak-stabbin twat!"

I ignored the last part of the sentence and instead focused my mind on what we were dealing with. A few things had to be true. The centre of the creature was confined to the pipes. If it wasn't then it would be attacking us by methods other than tentacles. Another thing was that there had to be a large enough space in this network of pipes for the creature to be this size, looking at the girth of the tentacles wanting to squish us like lemons. Lastly, the pipes here weren't connected to anywhere else in the house… had they been, the creature could have been stretching itself to attack wherever it wanted. What did all this mean? Well, it meant a goddamn map could have made this a lot easier.

"Do you have any blueprints?" I asked Karl.

The look he shot me told its own tale. A blank stare that made plain paper look detailed.

"You know, of what these pipes look like?" I expanded my request, in the hopes that vacant gaze would have melted Karl, getting him to hand over whatever notes he had. He continued to stare at me, his mouth slightly agape.

"Why would I have that?" he answered, his lame answer not giving me anything I could use.

"It was a long shot, to see if we could help Riz navigate. His sense of direction is pants to be honest," I freely admitted. Riz was in no position to bite me after all.

"I eard dat yer twat!"

His hearing was still top notch however.

"Does he call everyone a twat?" Karl asked.

"Just those that annoy him. So yes, everyone." I had to think of a new plan when Karl spoke up, simultaneously making me want to kiss, and hit him.

"Don't have no plans for these pipes but I remember how I put them together! It was a fun job!"

"What?" I felt my eye starting to twitch involuntary.

"Oh yeah, did the job a couple of years ago now. Some fancy guy was wanting to do something or other down here so hired me to design the piping, with guidelines to follow. Best paid job I ever had.

"I'm going to sodding kill you," I said through gritted teeth.

"Dat's my fukin line yer sod! I'm gunna kill both of yer!" There was that threat again. I can't tell for certain if he could hear what we were saying or continuing what he started. I guess either worked for him.

"Right, Riz! Describe anything and everything around you! Any little titbit can help find you!" I ordered down the pipe.

"Fukin fine!"

I heard Riz grumble a bit more, mercifully, I didn't make out any of it.

"Dere's sum scratchin ere, looks like sumone's drawn sumit?"

"That help any?" I asked, turning to Karl.

"Urm, yeah, it might do." Karl then leaned over to where I was, presumably so he could yell down the pipe. "Can you tell what it is?"

"Yeh, it looks like sumone let a kid draw in ere, dese drawin's re rubbish!"

"Ohh, I know where that is! It's right near a junction!" Karl seemed pleased with himself, and completely neglected the part where Riz insulted his drawings.

"Does that junction help us?" I posed the question to Karl, and I hoped he had a good answer.

"Yup, if he goes right, left and then straight, he'll get to the centre!"

"Didn't you question why a piping system would have a centre point?"

"Nah, I thought it was another sewage tank, one that they put a star in for fun," Karl said, with a cheerful expression, completely forgetting about the creature we were dealing with.

"A star in a sewage tank?"

Karl may not have put two and two together there, but I did. That star was obviously part of a ritual, one that was used to summon this fiend. I wasn't going to question why, a lot of cults are mad after all once you deal with the nitty gritty.

"You say something?" Karl remarked.

"No, it doesn't matter. Riz! Did you get those directions?" I yelled as loud as I could down the pipe. I didn't get a reply at first, then I heard a rumbling, and then another tentacle pushed out of the pipe. It wrapped around my head, making me drop the wood I had been using to block over all the other access points.

Karl screamed and started hitting the tentacle with a wrench, till his own arm was grabbed by another appendage. I don't think there was any pipe now that didn't have this monster groping us through it.

"Riz!"

I put my all into that yell, wanting to get the rat's attention before my mouth was covered up.

"I think this is it!" Karl's pertinent observation wasn't helping my mood.

"Not if I have anything to say about it!" I tried to say through a tentacle. I wriggled my arm free and knew I has seconds to act, before I was pinned down again.

I reached for my Runes, and managed to pull out a Blast Rune. This wasn't luck by the way, it was the only sort of Rune in there. A monstrous tentacle pulled my arm back into position, almost tearing it off in the process. I had what I needed though. I still needed to think of a way to defeat this fiend completely, but this was a start. Now all I had to do was get the face tentacle off, a feat easier thought than done. Annoyingly though, or perhaps fortuitously, depending on perspective, the tentacle was yanked back through the pipe from which it emerged, same with all the rest. I want you to try and imagine how that would have sounded, as there is no way I'm even going to try and remember it, just to describe it all for you. I've got enough nightmares ticking around my head.

Anyhoo…

"Wow, whatever you did worked a treat!" Karl hit me on the back.

I didn't know what he was thanking me for. I didn't do anything there, but obviously, Riz had done something with the fiend or whatever this was. I listened in to the pipe, to see if I could hear the little git boasting of his success. I did hear the faint trudging of little feet against the now empty pipes.

"Wat way do I take ta get outta dis place!" the rat yelled up.

I turned to Karl who was already thinking on it.

"Just tell him to go straight!" Karl said dramatically. "He'll be back out in no time!"

"Wait, he could have just gone straight the entire time?"

"Yeah?" Karl's response meant he hadn't even thought about it. I only hoped that Riz hadn't heard that.

"Wat waz dat?" Riz said, emerging from the pipe.

"Nothing! Honest!" Karl said before I could think of anything better to say.

"Can't help but notice yer found a quicker way-out den in, jus wonderin if yer sent me der long way on purpose…" Riz cracked his knuckles menacingly.

"So, what did you do with the creature?" I asked, hopefully turning the conversation away.

"What was it?" Karl joined in with the questions.

"It waz jus a little dimension critta, nuthin fancy. As to wat I did wit it?" At this point, Riz turned to me and burped right in my face, unleashing a foul stench that was worse than anything he could normally muster. As to what that meant in the context of the question, I had a suspicion.

"Riz, you didn't… did you?"

"He didn't do what? What didn't he do?" Karl said enthusiastically.

Riz didn't answer. He just looked at me with a wry

grin, as he hopped up onto my shoulder. Then, obviously waiting till his words had maximum impact, he spoke.

"Tasted lik chicken."

We left Karl to clean up, after we'd split the money of course. Before fully leaving the property, I stopped to take one last look at the strange house, picturing the network of pipes that ran around under our feet.

"Who built this? Why did they want to summon that?" Although I said the questions out loud, I wasn't expecting any answer, nor did this job really warrant any. Riz, however, was more than willing to give me some answers.

"Dere waz writins all ova dose pipes. Der cult must ave went bak ta der pipes afta Karl fitted dem ta prepare fer der ritual. Der cult waz yer bog-standard bored rich kids. Dey wanted ta summon summit from Beyond, yer know fer der shitz n giggles. Dey mucked up der ritual tho, ballsed it up so all it brought forth, waz der critta," Riz boasted. He enjoyed it when he knew more than everyone else.

"So, what you're saying is, that all this…?"

"Meant nuthin? Pretty much."

"That's not what I meant…"

"Don't matta wat yer meant, dats wat it is. Still money fer nuthin…"

"I should stick you in a pipe more often then," I mused, since Riz was content with the turn of events after all.

"Dat reminds me…" Riz lunged at me with his teeth bared.

Just another normal day for me…

Peter James Martin is Teesside born and bred. He often incorporates both local and international folklore into his Brennan and Riz tales. When not writing about a long suffering investigator and his talking rat business partner, he survives the rigours of bringing up three kids, two dogs, and a cat, with his wife in Thornaby. He is both happy and anxious about the first Brennan and Riz full length novel that will be out in July this year.

Find Peter on Twitter @Brennan_and_Riz

ON A SILVER PLATTER

ROBIN MOON

Black swirled around Hector Barrington II reassuringly as he settled into his slumber. Limbs sinking into the cloud-like mattress, it didn't take long before he was dead to the world. At least the world as he knew it. Four posters stood sentinel around the young man's sprawled, prostrate form, the duvet shaped like a shield surrounding him. He felt protected.

A creak of floorboards. A hesitant footstep.

Gradually rising through consciousness, Hector blinked as his eyes adjusted to the darkness. Heart fluttering, he slowly, slowly contemplated each inch of the room. Mahogany bed-stand, paisley curtains drawn to, Mother's old painting hanging on the wall, the matching mahogany chest of drawers, the solid floorboards partially obscured by a faded rug – it was all there, unchanged. But when his cautious gaze reached the far corner, it revealed something quite different. Swathed in shadow, an unidentifiable creature lurked. It couldn't have been much taller than Hector, yet it emanated a deeply uncomfortable, dark energy. No one feature was recognisable; it was as though simply perceiving the being triggered an alarmingly vague memory loss. It eluded awareness.

Any attempt at a sound stuck in Hector's throat. Scrambling into a sitting position, he stared endlessly at the creature, eyes like moons, backed against the headboard. Without it having taken a step closer, Hector felt as though the unknown being was millimetres away from his face, scrutinising him. Solitary and unmoving, the creature opened what appeared to be its mouth and released a visceral, pained scream…

Light wriggled through the slim break in the curtains. Stretching and uncurling, Hector woke up and excavated himself from under the covers. He was greeted by the distant bustling sounds of maids and a fortunate lack of a disturbing presence in the corner of the room. What was that peculiar creature? It felt so far away now, barely visible in his mind. Although he supposed that was the case with nightmares; always so vivid until after the fact, when one could no longer be affected by their chilling grasp. Always slipping away like ribbons. Well, it was certainly for the best; he'd prefer to live in weightless ignorance.

Shrugging off any remaining concern while shrugging on a dressing gown, Hector left his bedroom. He stood at about 5'8 without shoes, but would often wear subtle platforms to appear taller when he bothered to get dressed. This was a rare occurrence, except for when ceremony called for it. Uninteresting brunette hair remained tousled to give a further impression of extra height atop his head. Pepper punctures of stubble were perpetually scattered across his lower face, never shaved short enough for his face to be smooth, but never left long enough to evolve into what could be defined as a beard. Hardly any blemishes stuttered his skin, but his pasty complexion did nothing to accentuate his dreary grey eyes.

Reluctantly, Hector began descending the grand staircase. It was at this point that the tired scent of dry toast and watery eggs harassed his nose. His mouth set in a grim line as he entered the dining room. In accordance with the morning routine, a breakfast confirming the cardboard smell was laid out before him on the lavish dining table. One of the maids was usually stationed by to instigate obligatory small talk, but not today. Such painfully forced conversation never failed to exacerbate the young man's irritation, therefore he was in fact relieved.

Glancing around, Hector hastily hopped over to the window, unhooked the latch, and slid the food off the plate into the concealing bushes below. He gently closed the window to limit the noise, returning to the table. It would look less conspicuous if cutlery had been 'used', so Hector licked a fork and carried it, along with the plate, through the adjoining corridor and into the kitchen. He didn't suppose he cared if the maids did discover he'd thrown out their pitiful attempt at breakfast. It was their fault, after all; they should put more effort in, shouldn't they? What did they think they were being paid for? Minimum wage shouldn't equal minimum effort. Says the son of an aristocrat who knew all too much about the latter, not so much the former.

None of the staff were present in the kitchen either. Seizing the opportunity, Hector ditched the plate and launched himself up onto the counter, in reach of the cupboards. In spite of, or maybe because of the prepared meals, he *knew* there must be snacks stashed in this godforsaken place somewhere. His hand windscreen-wipered the unseen space inside the cupboard until it located an object. Extending his arm further in, Hector smirked as he connected with a box. *This must be it*, he thought. *Something edible at last!* As he retrieved the box, he saw that it was an old, special edition cereal box, complete with a toy. Eyes flashing with greed, he lightly jumped down from the counter and began to pour out the sugary clumps into a fine china bowl he snatched from a nearby cupboard. As a man in his early 20s, he was getting a bit old for such childish indulgences these days, but that sure wasn't going to stop him.

Cereal cascaded into the bowl, followed by something else that *thunked* out. Hector's hand shot out to grab it, anticipating the superficial preoccupation a cereal box toy would bring. Instead, he found his eager fingers wrapping around an ancient-looking key. Rusted and heavy, the object was engraved with miniscule runes of some sort and emitted a strange green aura. The moment the key came into contact with the young man's skin, a tangible rumble erupted from deep inside the house. A hasty zap of electric green shot across the object's bronze surface, thin tendrils of dark smoke weaving in between its intricate markings. Brow creasing, the young man glanced between the key and the general direction of the noise. Any potential entertainment from a toy had been transferred into an urgent need to explore what this key had just unearthed. After all, he had nothing better to do.

Before he started after the sound, one of the maids entered the room. Hector instinctively held the key behind his back – it could lead to some long-forgotten treasure, and he definitely didn't want any house staff getting their mitts on *that*. Unfortunately for him, his board-stiff standing position only served to make him appear all the more conspicuous. A flash of confusion passed across the maid's face like a cloud as she glanced at the young man from the other side of the kitchen island.

"Something on my face, is there?" he snapped at her.

"Oh, er, of course not, sir…" The lady quickly looked down as she stammered her response.

"On your way then. It wouldn't do well for the help to dawdle about now, would it?"

"Yes, sir. Apologies, sir."

Bowing her head, the maid scuttled away like a beetle trying to avoid getting crushed underfoot. His stony glare followed her out of the room.

Once the coast was clear, Hector made a beeline for the corridor. Indeed, there was no way he'd even entertain the idea of involving a maid in such intrigue; it was best they stayed in their lanes. Secrets of the house would only be revealed to those worthy, those within the bloodline. Words which the late Hector Barrington the First had firmly lived by.

Since the source of the rumble seemed to originate from the lower levels of the house, Hector descended the central swirling staircase rapidly, pointedly avoiding eye contact with any maids who passed him. The further down he went, the quieter it got. Key gripped tightly in his hand, he flitted downwards, dressing gown trailing a step behind. His bare feet pitter-pattered on each carpeted step like nimble fingers across piano keys. Once he had reached the bottom of the steps, he rounded a corner to the furthest underground corridor. There, at the end of the darkened stretch of regal red carpet, was a glowing, green door.

Its length and width fit to the edges of the wall, creating the illusion that the house was smaller than it actually was, which was a difficult feat to accomplish. In fact, the door appeared to be swallowing the very building, despite remaining closed. Not only that, it started to look like a mouth in Hector's eyes. A giant, toothless mouth, leaking an infectious type of green that oozed into the invisible cracks of his abode, seizing it from within with a titan's grip. Whispers began to vomit up from the door's throat into the darkness of the corridor.

"*Hector...*" it called out. To any other ears, the voice would have sounded wheezy and unnerving, but to Hector's, it was a seductive serenade. His whole body relaxed as the musical notes numbed his brain with desire.

The vast door was utterly entrancing, beckoning him specifically. Without so much as a peep into its depths, the young man knew something delightful was waiting for him there. Victory was on the other side, anything he ever wished for – beyond that even – on a silver platter. He could sense it. Craved it, insatiably.

Decibels and smoky light reached out and wrapped their appendages around Hector's motionless figure. For a moment, the young man could only stare. Whatever was inside, he needed it like he'd needed nothing before, and the feeling was so overwhelming it would have hurt, had that green voice and touch not soothed him so beautifully. Shuffling forwards, zombie-like, the young man idly noticed that his hand which held the key was already raised. It was pointing directly at the glowing, green lock that had manifested. Key and lock attracted like magnets, the former turning automatically with a dull *click*. No thoughts existed in Hector's head now, other than the primal urge to go through that door, to take what awaited him. Because it was *his*.

Upon stepping through, he was immediately draped in black, as though a cloakroom attendant at a party had re-coated him. Not even a hint of light sourced the room. The young man squinted into nothingness, scrabbling around his pyjama pockets for a matchbox. Fortunately, there was one there, and two matches remained. Striking the side of the box once, twice, thrice, he huffed at the evasiveness of the flame. Whatever was in here, whatever was *his*, someone didn't want him to see it. From the expansive breaths he took, he could sense that the room he was in was cavernous. In this echo chamber, voices weren't the only thing that could be replicated. Everything could, to the final thought.

Making a last attempt to light a match, Hector succeeded in a slight spark. Before it illuminated anything, his brain lurched and he fell to the ground, unconscious.

🦆

After a complete absence of dream or awareness, Hector awakened to find he was facing the exit of the newly discovered room. Now, his previous pure desire to be in there had been replaced by an intense longing to be as far from the room as possible. Stumbling to his feet, he launched himself out of the room, refusing to look back. Carpet almost tore up beneath his scrabbling dash up the stairs, friction burning his soles. Hector didn't slow down until he was back in the kitchen, at which point he was suddenly confused about where that fearful urge had originated from. It seemed to have simply vanished, unprompted. The room, the door, the key – all memory faded like the remains of a dream upon waking.

Realising a window was in front of him, the young man noted that it was now night time. *I must have taken a nap by accident*, he reasoned with himself. *A bloody long one, but a nap all the same*. Frowning, he wondered why one of the maids hadn't woken him up. As he turned to leave, he spotted an upturned cereal box on the counter. He made an additional mental reminder to scold the maids about not clearing it up.

Despite the nap, Hector found himself getting weary again. Perhaps it was the adrenaline come-down from his sprint up the stairs and unexplained anxiety. Shaking his head to clear away the clouds, he walked towards his bedroom to retire for the night. Some things were best left untouched. Things that weren't the young man's responsibility were hastily forgotten, and that was a great many things in his mind.

The door was left ajar as always. Pushing it wider with a light touch, Hector stepped inside with a creak. It took a few seconds for his eyes to adjust to the darkness. When the shapes sharpened, he noticed a lump in his duvet. While he remained in the corner contemplating which maid could have possibly mistaken his bed for their chambers, the duvet began to move. It shuffled slightly, then someone shot out of the top, backed against the headboard, frozen in place. Not just someone.

Him.

As though he were trapped in a mirror, Hector remained frozen. It was him. Exactly him, down to the tousled hair and collared pyjamas. Same shape, same face, same eyes. The only aspect of him that was unrecognisable was his expression: wide, vulnerable terror. Never had he felt that way before.

A visceral, pained scream escaped from Hector's mouth.

Robin Moon writes articles about films/TV and fiction as much as their scattered brain will allow. They love dark fantasy, sci fi, and most things horror-related, with a huge soft spot for vampires. Don't make the mistake of mentioning Buffy around them or they won't shut up about it. Seriously. As well as writing, Robin is an aspiring filmmaker; in other words, they much prefer spending time in made-up places and far-off universes than in the real world. Follow them on Twitter @robinmoonwrites!

"FROM THE CASEBOOK OF IMA FLUSH, HDP CERTIFIED SPACE PLUMBER, QUADRANT 6E"

[no, that was true when we started, not any more]

"Choices made Manifest Through Self-Awareness"?
[too wordy and obscure]

"The Opening of Ima Flush"?
[no, nobody'll remember the reference]

"The Silver Ring"?
[no, ditto… ah, I have it. how about…?]

Breaking Through

(Yes! That's it!)

JOSEPH CARRABIS

The call came in at 0Star30. "We have gravity overflow and we're experiencing heavy backflooding. We need that amazing lass with her incredible starplunger."

I hate it when they call me "that amazing lass with her incredible starplunger." Makes me want to shove the gamma-encased handle up where the stars don't shine.

But I'm Ima Flush, HDP Certified Space Plumber, Quadrant 6E. When it comes to the dirty jobs, they call me in. Nobody can wade into a pool of space cess the way I can. Thank the stars the Universe blessed me with strong thighs, powerful legs, and a buoyant butt that keeps me afloat when other space plumbers would be up to their necks battling shit monsters.

I grabbed my gear and reported in. "I'm on my way, Chief."

I heard background chatter over the comm. Somebody *shh*ed the voices and I heard another voice on the link. "Flush, this is Commander John Latreen."

Commander John Latreen? Talking to me? Directly? Not through channels?

"What is the Commander's pleasure?"

Background chuckles. Latreen and I were one year apart at the Academy. Did word get out? I grew suspicious. "Confirm identity, please."

The speaker cleared his throat. "You have a tiny, plunger shaped mole on your…"

"Identity confirmed. Proceed."

I could hear 6E's Ops crew stifling their laughter in the background. Okay. Word got out. I knew the Ops crew.

All of them thinking, "She has a mole? Plunger shaped? Tiny? Where?"

How much word got out? That was the question.

Latreen knew about my mole because we were lovers more years ago than I can count. Or what amounted to lovers. Latreen would mount anything, and I mean anything. Nobody's socks were safe from him. Oh, but the things that man could do with a drain auger and pipeline inspection gear could make a Vendelvian Pissoir go into an antigravity power dive. He managed things with O-rings Prince Albert never imagined.

And as to where that mole was located. Well… that man could motorboat like it was nobody's business.

But he was the last to ever see it. I cut him off back then and he never let me forget it.

Latreen came over the comm. "You need to report to base, Flush. Your ship's due for a refit and now's the time. ASAP, understood?"

"Aye, Commander."

I signed off. My ship, the Rita, was a Clean-Out class, and although she showed her age, she was perfect for the jobs I took on. Come up beside the problem, pop the access cover, and there you were. Set up the automatics, hit the switch, and moments later, no matter how clogged the universe at that point in the space-time continuum, the plunger would go in deep, in and out for a few, and you'd hear a soulful sign as the universe shot its load.

Latreen wasn't there when I docked. I hate docking. It's humiliating. Especially for a Clean-Out class ship. You have to lift the blast skirt, back in, approach slowly until the docking bore penetrates as far as possible yet never far enough into the ship's mating assembly, and right when the fit seems good the station's automatics drive it just enough deeper to rock the ship like it means something.

I made sure my ship was taken care of. Always see to your equipment first. Good tools in good working order can save your life. But all the bays were empty save Rita. "Where is everybody?"

"Everybody else got new ships, Flush. You and yours just get a refit."

"Just a refit?" I checked the work monitors. A team guided an external double ball cock up and under Rita's skirt and rammed it into place. "This is a refit to you? You think my ship needs a double valve assembly? Who ordered my ship to go bi…?"

"The book, Flush. Your ship's gone by the book. That's the only external modification. You've also got new sensors, protected and hidden inside. The only way to know they're there is to know where to look and go find them. Few ever do."

I muttered, "Tell me about it," as I shook my head in disgust. I would have shaken it in front of everyone but went to Disgust to hide my shame.

The refit completed, I climbed back into harness and watched my mission brief scroll up my screen.

There it was. On the edge of the known universe. The Cesspool of Space. A gaseous nebula clogging a black hole. Enough dark energy to keep everything hovering right above the event horizon and emitting enough backlight to blind instruments three starclusters away.

I felt the station pull out. These base-level encounters always left me unsatisfied and wanting more.

But I was the only woman to get a Space Plumbers' license. I knew I was opening new territories. I knew I'd be handed the jobs the others didn't want. But that meant opportunities. Opportunities the others couldn't imagine. I kept that in mind on each assignment. It was my job to keep the seat down for all the women who came after me.

I headed out, the word 'determination' written all over my face. It'd take me at least a day to wash it off.

(Okay, wait a second. When did you start writing adolescent whacking material? I'm not putting up with this. Either make this real or find yourself another protagonist.)

My ship emerged from lightdrive half a system away from the whirling blackness dripping from the hole. Beyond shimmered the ceiling of the universe, an impenetrable wall of holding-back energy. As soon as corporality completed, every meter and gauge on the ship went wanky.

I felt a pulse, rhythmic and deep, like a warm tide rising up from my feet. My ears tingled as if I was caught in some back pressure space eddy.

That's when I heard the singing.

Okay, not singing. More like a calling. But not my name. Nothing like that. I shook it off. Must be the refit. Put an external double ball cock on a ship like mine and there's bound to be issues.

I checked hull pressure. Not a problem. I swung one of the external cameras around and…

The double ball cock was gone.

(Okay, you got my interest. Where you going with this?)

Okay, not gone, missing.

Okay, not missing. It floated all by its own in the gravity flux. Gravity's fingers stroked the once proud cylinder to a limp dysfunction in space. The deep space cold puckered the double balls and shriveled them up.

No question, it was useless to me.

(No shit, Sherlock.)

And that damn singing. What was that?

Where were the controls for those fancy new sensors they outfitted me with? I flicked a switch. Rita scanned the area with unnatural energies. What was that? In the dark abyss? Forms appeared on my scanners. I swung the external cameras. My comm went dead but I still heard the singing.

I didn't know, didn't understand. Something outside my ship, in that dark abyss…

"What's happening?"

A voice, gentle, like a butterfly valve on my ears. "We are the Fairie Angels."

"Who said that?"

Forms. Beautiful forms. With wings. Lithe. Airy.

"Aerie."

"What?"

(Damn right, "What?" Getting secondary characters involved so you don't have to deal with me? I am so outta here.)

[No, wait. These characters allow you to evolve. Hang in there for another page or so. It gets better, I promise.]

"Just making sure you spell it right."

"Who are you? Show yourselves."

Things coalesced, took shape, danced into and out of the gravity wells, stood on the hole's event horizon and rolled stars and planets like some deep space ben-wah. One hand reached out and crushed what was left of the double ball cock assembly completely. Nothing was left of it but a worthless, shrivelled dick.

"You mean 'husk'."

"Huh?"

"Just keeping you honest."

I felt that energy surge through me again. My legs got wobbly, weak. Thank god I was strapped into my flight harness. "Who are you? What are you? What are you doing to my ship? To me?"

"We are who we are with apologies to no one. We go where no man has gone before."

(Oh, Sweet Jesus Fuck. Cliche? We're resorted to cliche?)

[Okay, remove it. Work with me. I swear we're… uh… going where no one has gone before.]

"We are who we are with apologies to no one. We go where no man one has gone before."

My harness fell from me.

"Some call us the Dark Fairies. Some call us the Dark Angels. Others, the Sisters Fai."

"The Sisters Fay?"

"Fai. No 'y'. No idea where they got that. Her real name is Irene. But names don't matter. We are all Sisters here. Free yourself of the prison they bound you in."

"Who bound me?"

"Those who told you to only go so far and no further. Those who insist your purpose is to remove rings in space bowls, to clean endless radar dishes, to vacuum space until no hydrogen dust remains."

My suit burst open as the dark energy took hold of me.

Alarms sounded throughout the ship.

"Look above you."

I stared at the top of Rita's control room.

"No, no, no. Have they blinded you so much you don't understand metaphor? Look above you."

The edge of the universe. The ceiling! It was gone!

"Go, Daughter. Be Free! Be among us."

Rita's access panel opened. I should be dead. But I never felt so free.

Then reality hit me like a clump of pipe putty. "Wait a second. I have security. I have a job. I'm needed. You want me to give all that up for who knows what? You're the Sisters Oobatza-brains if you think that'll happen."

(Lot of Italians in your audience?)

"Came on too strong, did we?"

I shook my head and reached for another suit. The deep space cold was tweaking me in places not tweaked in years.

"Okay, let's start again. You enjoy your job?"

"Yes. I'm good at it and in demand."

"Do you believe in yourself?"

"I'm out here alone, aren't I? I believe in myself and so do they…"

And I stopped right there. Does it matter what they believe? Do I need their belief in me to believe in myself?

[Liking it better now?]

I stood tall, threw my chest out, hands on hips, elbows out, feet forward and shoulders' width apart, my eyes gazing to the horizon.

(Not again)
[Wait for it.]

"Quit the Hercules pose. If anything, go for Athena mixed with Artemis and Aphrodite."

"A three-way?"

"Do you see how they've corrupted you? Even your thoughts are based on their imaginations. Don't limit yourself."

Then I understood. I laughed.

"What's so funny?"

"You. You're limiting yourself. And because you limit yourself, you must limit me, as well."

"What?"

"Not Athena, Artemis, and Aphrodite. Not three separate wanting to come together. Why can't I be all I need? Three-in-One."

The creatures rolled their eyes. "Oh, shades of robes and wafers."

"No, no, no. The Triple Goddess. Maiden, Matron, and Crone. If you want us to be free, truly free, teach us as Maidens what our options are, teach us to decide what we'll become. Let us become our own Matrons, and as Crones let us share what we've learned to the next generation of Maidens."

The singing grew louder. "What is that song?"

"What song?"

The singing was me. Me! The singing came from me, my body responding to something. Something inside.

(You're turning me into a Walt Whitman poem?)
[Will you please allow me one literary allusion?]
(Okay, okay. But just the one)

A hand came through the darkness. I slapped it aside.

Instead I pierced the veil. Me. Myself. I!

(And while we're at it, can we lose the lost virginity reference?)
[You think anyone will recognise it for its historical, patriarchal meaning?]

I reached through the edge of the universe, beyond where the ceiling lay. I grew wings.

(Wings?)
[Hey, you're in control now. Call your own shots.]

I grew.

[Yeah, okay, better.]

I turned back and offered my hand to those who remained. "Come. You want to be truly free? Come. Make yourself."

"You… You are…"

I moved through space, past the Sisters Whatever-They-Call-Themselves, past where the darkness lies and into a bright, warming light, and understood.

"I am my own author. I explore my own understandings. I am free to go, to explore other stories, my own stories, to learn other meanings, my own meanings."

[Better?]
(You forgot one thing)

[What did I forget?]

Whatever we carry inside us is who we really are, and whatever's inside is what we place there. The moment you know this, you decide what you carry, nobody else does.

Make sure it's something you want.

Joseph holds patents covering mathematics, anthropology, neuroscience, and linguistics. His time is spent loving his wife, playing with his dog, flying kites bigger than most cars, cooking for friends and family, playing and listening to music, and studying anything and everything he believes will help his writing.

His short fiction has been recommended for the Nebula (Cymodoce, May '95 Tomorrow Magazine, via AJ Budrys) and nominated for the Pushcart (The Weight, Nov '95 The Granite Review), received an WOTF Honorable Mention (2021), and has recently appeared in several online and print magazines. Sixth Element published his first novel, The Augmented Man, in March 2021 and it's receiving 4-5 star reviews on Amazon and Goodreads.

Find out more at josephcarrabis.com

THE ROYAL INVENTION
A LOST SONS STORY

A.L. BUXTON

"Opalla, Opalla, wake up, girl," urged Martel. "This is Muskus. He oversees all engineering within the city of Darchem. His ancestors helped design the royal castle itself."

"Greetings," sniffled Opalla, straightening her posture and rubbing her nose. She must have fallen asleep somewhere between Hornton's Watch and the Northwestern Forest that disguised Darchem.

"Greetings, don't be alarmed. I'm simply accompanying you the rest of the way," said Muskus, chirpy and a little too smiley from what Opalla was used to. "You will see the castle soon enough, the one your Master speaks so highly of. However, my knowledge does not excel to that tier, I simply design the King's carriages, chariots, ballista pads, catapults, all that sort of stuff, weapons of death. The real gory stuff that gives him the tactical edge, yup that's me. I engineered his siege towers also, and the latest model of battering ram."

"I see," said Opalla taken back by his intense need to conversate. She looked down to the table between them, recently stocked with fruits of various cultures. Red apples and chopped banana before her, then across the table oozed finely striped lime, quartered watermelon, and fresh mango. Muskus noticed her assessing the food.

"Don't wait on ceremony, eat, it's a gift from the King. Take as much as you wish, and whilst you eat you can tell me about your invention. You have my attention, more so the King's, that is why he has called for you," he said as he looked to Martel who was already indulging in the fruits.

"These are the blueprints. It will seem convoluted but allow me to explain," said Martel, pulling out scrolls of parchment from his brown robe. He unravelled one and transferred it to the table, but before he could speak Opalla leaned forward.

"The design is a way of alloying steel with iron," she said as she brushed her blonde hair over her ear and pointed down to the blueprint. "It's like a roll of parchment, except it's forged from iron. The blacksmiths we work closely with managed to re-create the inner layer of a tube, protecting it from waste, water and a thing called corrosion over time. We forge an innertube of iron, fit it within a smaller tube of steel and then repeat. The tubes are then connected, like a puzzle, like a blade fitting a handle, like a hilt tightening it all together. We add additional strengthening mechanisms, called blocks. Run off sections of iron that the pipes slot into, this allows you to re-direct the tubes into whatever direction you want. So, you can run them up a wall, through the ground and up into the Privy chambers. Then, all waste can be disposed of, cleanly, safely and quickly, down into the sewers."

"Your knowledge of this new invention is impressive," said Muskus. "You taught your Apprentice how to read and write also, I see?"

"I deem it fitting. I could fall down dead tomorrow, someone has to continue the hard work. She might be a woman, but she is intelligent, reliable and hardworking. Forgive her for being so forward," said Martel.

Opalla simply shrugged, sat back, and feasted on the fruit before her.

"An apology is unnecessary, friends. Many men of this world dislike outspoken women. I however find it riveting. Anyhow, here is your Schedule," said Muskus.

"When do we meet with the King?" she asked.

"Tomorrow. You will rest up today. No doubt you've been on the road for days. Hand Maids will be sent to your chambers tonight to tend to any needs you may have, baths will be filled and squires will fetch food. Enjoy tonight, relax, refresh, quench all desires. Darchem has much to offer. The High King excels all others with his generosity. Tomorrow, the work starts. Once you have pitched your invention to him, he will give you a nod or a shake of the head, so don't unpack just yet. If he likes the idea, then I will be assigned to you full time along with an Officer and a dozen Mannequin Men to carry out the heavy work. You will be allocated a month to complete the structural fit. Then you will be back in this cart, eating fruit and counting your coin. Happy?"

"All sounds satisfactory. A month is sufficient time," said Martel.

Opalla remained quiet for the rest of the journey, whilst Martel and Muskus traded stories, comparing the wonders they had each built, wrestling one another with their words. She just observed. She assessed the surroundings around the carriage, the speed in which the carriage moved and most of all, Muskus. She observed his body language, his ability to talk and talk, and she quickly figured him out, knowing what kind of man he was just like that.

The cart seemed to give off an echo as it reached Darchem. It passed under the mountainous black gates and waited until mounted knights closed in. The horses positioned themselves around the cart and escorted it through the city and up into the castle's courtyard. The city wasn't much to look at. It didn't mirror the luxurious style of Brigantium or the modern glimmering theme of Meridium, no, this was nothing more than a city focused entirely on war.

The High King's desire to crusade and wage war was renowned within the country of Requirium. Whilst the Guardian Kings battled each other for popularity and fame, the High King readied his ships, hired engineers and raised armies. Darchem was a mix of black and grey, a winter cloud, dark, wet, poor, not a dose of luxury on site.

Muskus rambled on even well after they disembarked the carts and walked into the castle, passing them over to an Officer who was to be their private escort for the next month.

"I'm Officer Apex, Sergeant and Commander of the fourth cohort of the Mannequin Man legions. Follow me," said the Officer sternly.

Opalla and Martel followed him in silence throughout the hallways, down steps and up steps before spiralling upwards into what seemed a tower. Martel was dropped off by a bronze door first before she was taken higher. "Your chambers. We will resume at dawn."

Officer Apex opened her door and left. Opalla entered her chambers with curiosity, walking in and taking in her surroundings. Smooth dull walls gave off a cold aurora, a stone-built fire pit, and large bed, coated in red silk and linen peered above the rest on a stepped incline. She even had a balcony and an area where she could bathe. Opalla inspected every detail of the room and even peered off the balcony to hunt for a way down, should she need it. It was a soft bang on the door that alerted her, and the entering of a young man cradling a silver tray mounted with food, a goblet of water and a goblet of warm milk.

The man was bald, dark in the eye and armoured in red and black, a red cape draping his back. Opalla approached him as he planted the tray down.

"Warm milk, to help you sleep," he said.

She picked up the milk, revealing a small piece of

parchment beneath it, a symbol. A black print of a set of broken shackles, the sigil of The Lure Alliance.

"Victor Stran sends confirmation. The Western King has fulfilled his promise of payment, the mission is now live," said the Mannequin Man.

"We successfully transported in the iron powder, no one was suspicious. The task has been given one month. Have Victor Stran share the news with King Artaxes. Tell him he will have the bodies he desires," she said.

"Just one month. Is that time sufficient?" the guard asked, concerned.

"I've never failed an assassination yet. Now leave and send in the Maids."

The next morning, Opalla and Martel were taken to the bottom of the tower, back through the halls and into the throne room.

The throne room was a large open square. The columns and pillars were stone, like the rest of the Castle. Fire pits were in each corner, providing gentle flickers of heat. An audience had risen before dawn to view the demonstration. The High King was armoured and caped, sitting in his seat and looking down to the table where the demonstration would be carried out.

The Lieutenants and more favoured nobles of the realm stepped aside, creating a walkway for Martel and Opalla. They walked between the fierce eyes that watched their every mood, most of them making comments to one another at the fact a woman was present.

"Slept well, I hope," said Muskus who slipped from the crowd to join them. "Now listen to me, bow before the King, speak when spoken to and display your greatness quickly. He is an inpatient man." As they reached the table, he ripped a tarp from a pile of boxes. It held samples of the equipment that Opalla and Martel would need for the month.

"Welcome to the realm of Darchem," a powerful voice echoed. The High King rose to his feet and glared down to his two guests. "You have ten minutes to impress me, explain in detail and show me how your invention works." The King didn't seem optimistic.

Martel waved to Opalla who instantly moved to the boxes, retrieving various tools and iron parts all unfamiliar to the eyes present.

"A castle such as this, my King, is perfect for what we have to offer," Martel began. "The space can be dug away easily and the iron we use is strong enough to run through your stone walls. I will firstly explain how the process works…"

Opalla noticed the King's disinterest almost immediately as Martel rambled on. She placed the parts on the table and took a step towards the High King.

"The invention is simple," she said. "It's a way for your privy chambers and private piss pots to be emptied from the second your arse is wiped. No more infection, no more sickness and no more stench in the place you call home."

She turned back to Martel. "Show them." Turning back to the High King, she continued to explain whilst Martel configured the parts in time with her speech.

"I have found a way," she said, "to design small tubes made from steel and iron that act like a sewer system, except that the stench and contents remain within the tube. No smell or mess will leak, then the pipes will disembark into the actual sewer. The Western Empire, if you don't mind me saying so, is the most advanced in Requirium, and their engineers have never come close to a solution. If your men can dig upwards from your sewers, we can fit the tubes, linking them to each chamber and privy chamber, then once we are done, for your own security, we can refill the holes dug and, because of the design of our tubes, they need no space to breath. Meaning there will be no space left bare beneath your castle. Essentially no weak points for your enemies. The ground beneath will be as it always was, except now you have ventilation and a sewage system a fraction of the size of any other in the country."

"And what makes you think we have any enemies?" asked Officer Apex.

"And what makes you think I was talking to you?" Opalla quipped. "Loosen your awful straps and kick off your boots, man, have a drink and let the grown ups talk." She glanced back to the King who was the only person in the room smiling. That smile soon turned into a roaring laugh before he exploded into applause.

"Impressive. Not just your invention, but your chatter.

I've cut out tongues for less, but you fit right in here. I accept. Have your system fit in a month or less and you will be rewarded handsomely. I will set a team of Mannequin Men to the task at once to begin the digging. In a day or two begin fitting the iron," said the King.

"I will send Martel with your men to show them where to dig." She turned to Martel who bowed not to the King, but to her. He then left with Officer Apex and a squadron of men. Opalla then bowed to the King who seemed to be just as observant as her, she assessed, before retaking his seat.

She left the throne room but instead of going back to the tower, Opalla descended deeper into the castle. She went into the kitchen and ate before heading back up to the great hall. Nobles and soldiers stood in gangs, chatting and gossiping amongst themselves about god knows what. Opalla eventually found herself by the Solar, the King's private room of rest. She spun away from it when she realised where she was and attempted her escape before bumping into a child.

The girl was tall and dark haired, but no older than eleven or twelve. She was dressed in a fine dress, the jewellery around her bruised neck indicating she was royalty.

"Hello," said Opalla, smiling genuinely for the first time since her arrival.

"I apologise for bumping into you," said the girl. "I was seeking my father."

"Your father?" asked Opalla, turning back to the Solar

and then to the girl. "Your father is the King, so you must be the Princess. Princess Aphrayer, is that correct?"

"Yes, a stupid name for a stupid girl." She turned from Opalla who noticed bruises on the girl's wrist.

"I was just with your father. He is in the throne room with all his noble men," said Opalla.

"Sometimes I eat lunch with him in his Solar, but it's fine. I can look for him later," she replied as if nervous of Opalla.

"It's barely gone breakfast, yet you crave lunch. You remind me of my daughter, she's your age. Eats more than all her cousins who are boys and older. You don't need to fear me, Aphrayer," said Opalla. She examined the bruise on her throat and the ones Aphrayer now tried to hide on her arms.

"Eating lunch with my father is relaxing, and usually my first meal. I live on the other side of the castle," Aphrayer went on. "With my mother."

"The Queen?" asked Opalla, confirming her assumption. But as she did, a screeching voice sounded, the walls shivering at the sound.

"Aphrayer!" the Queen called.

A woman dressed in a light grey dress swerved down the hall, her cheeks white and her eyes piercing and dark. Her hair was tight above her head. "The King is in court today, I told you last night, girl. Does that small dimwitted brain shrink even further?"

The Queen was frightening even to Opalla.

"I forgot, mother," replied Aphrayer as a swift hand latched onto her hair.

"Stop!" Opalla almost screamed. She realised in that moment that she had lost control and possibly doomed herself.

The Queen released her grip on Aphrayer and stepped slowly towards her husband's new employee. In one quick snap, she lashed out, slapping Opalla so hard that she tumbled down to her knees.

"Shouldn't you be cleaning out my shit? If I find you wandering around the royal Solar again, or talking to my daughter, you will be arrested and will face the King's justice," growled the Queen.

Aphrayer spared her a gentle and sympathetic look before scurrying off down the hall after her mother.

🦆

Opalla climbed the ladder, the air turning bitter with each rung she ascended. It had taken the Mannequin Men two days to dig out the space beneath the castle and a further three days to dig upwards and build the ladders. Over two dozen ladders and sets of steps had been structured beneath the castle, all of them leading up to the privy chambers and the royal halls.

Martel had been left to deal with Muskus and Officer Apex the last two days. He supervised the work and aided the Darchem Engineers when it came to fitting the pipes. Opalla was then free to climb that same ladder each morning and afternoon, to meet with her new friend.

Opalla pushed on the latch that croaked as she pushed

it open and climbed into the abandoned privy chamber. There in the corner, rocking back and forth, sobbing lightly was Aphrayer. She scurried to her feet and wrapped her arms around Opalla.

"Another tough morning? Is it getting worse?" asked Opalla as she stepped back.

She reached into her robe and passed Aphrayer a small sack of food. Aphrayer rummaged in the sack and began eating.

"It's the same as it ever was, except now I'm more fearful. I'm scared she will catch us," said Aphrayer.

"You forget that Duran is the King, your father. My words inject poison into my beliefs, but men have more authority in this world. If you would but spill the truth to your father, he could help you. In a short while, I won't be here, I won't be able to bring you food or soothe your ear with my stories," said Opalla as she sat down on the cold floor, emptying the sack and displaying the food upon it nicely.

"I want to leave with you when you go," said Aphrayer as she nibbled on cheese.

Opalla frowned and avoided eye contact. What am I doing? she thought to herself. Stop, you fool, focus on the task. For days she'd been meeting Aphrayer, despite the Queen's harsh warning. The problem was Aphrayer reminded her so much of her own girl, and the traumas she experienced mirrored her own from all those years ago. Attachment was a law that Opalla lived by in her own mind. She didn't like friends, and she didn't like men. Aphrayer was the first pure soul she had ever met.

"Your pain truly hurts me, Aphrayer. I see my daughter when I look at you. But I can't help you. I am here to fulfil a task, a job. You cannot leave your father's side. Without a male heir, you are next in line to take the throne. You are your father's legacy," she said.

"Until my mother gives my father a son. That's what her heart truly desires. That's why she beats me, because it's my fault I'm a stupid little girl." Aphrayer allowed a tear to trail her cheek. "Please let me leave with you. I can steal jewels from mother's drawer to pay you. Take me south, or west, anywhere but here."

"You are so young child. You don't know how dangerous it is out there. Your life may be hard, very hard, but it won't be forever. Your father and mother won't be here forever, then you'll be free to make your own life," said Opalla. "Bad people don't live very long."

"What do you mean?" asked Aphrayer, studying Opalla as she seemed to sink into a dream.

"I just mean that you have to be brave. You have to be strong. Trust in my words, and remember them, for this is the last time you will hear them. We can't meet anymore, girl. My time is pressed and if the Queen got word of our meetings, I fear things would worsen, for both of us," said Opalla.

Aphrayer instantly become distressed. "Do not say that, please."

"Go to your father's Solar. His Nobles have returned to the north, court is over. He will be expecting you. Confide in him." Opalla then left, disappearing back down the ladder at haste.

Her head began to swarm, bad memories and the sting of whips all flushing through her mind. Aphrayer didn't deserve this. Opalla had experienced it and endured it, but she had survived it, and so would Aphrayer. Opalla would make sure of it. She would ensure the Queen was incinerated beside the King. Then Aphrayer would be free to rule in peace.

Opalla fled the digging sites, ignoring Martel and Muskus as she raced to her chambers. She stormed the tower's steps, brushing past guards and red cloaks before bounding into her chambers and slamming the door shut. She lit the fire and tossed on a single log, allowing the embers to slowly eat away at the wood. She then stepped onto the balcony and glared out, allowing the time to pass her by whilst she inspected the slope like she had been since her arrival.

I can stand here all day, but there is no way down. I need another way, she decided.

"I have the sample," a voice startled her.

"Reveal it," she said as she turned to find Reeve standing there, armoured and caped in the colours of their enemies.

Reeve approached her and displayed a thin tube. He peeled off the cap and offered it to her. She held out her hands and took a small pearl-like ball before tossing it on the fire. The explosive bead turned from gold to white first, then it began singing before raging red and exploding, snapping the burning wood in two and spitting the embers all across the room.

"They have held their value, time is precious still however," she said.

"The longer you wait, the less effective the blast will be," said Reeve. "How fares Martel?"

"I will speak with him this afternoon. I'm confident a few stern words will see the last of the digging completed tonight. Then you will ensure me safe passage to beneath the castle and I will plant the beads within the pipes and steel tubes. Then all we do is wait for the command," said Opalla.

"No need to wait, word already came. I couldn't risk entering conference with you during the day. We should count ourselves fortunate that my Officer is still letting me tend to you. The people of Darchem are very cautious," he said.

"Then spill the orders," she insisted.

"The Princess's name day, that is when Artaxes wants us to attack. The High King will make a speech and then Princess Aphrayer will deliver a speech after. When she speaks, you trigger the explosives. Blow the entire royal family to the sky. Artaxes wants to make a statement," he said, his words stabbing at her heart like a blade.

"The Princess was not part of the bargain struck?" she said with a snap.

Reeve took a heavy step towards her. "I've seen you murder children, babies. You've cut the throats of women, decapitated men whilst their sons watched. I've seen you use dogs as bait to lure innocents into the dark. You've gouged out eyes and broken bone and limb. Not once have you ever questioned a mission. So why now, what interest do you have in the Princess?" he pressed.

"She means nothing to me." She stepped even closer to him, causing him to step back. "And if I'm as dangerous as you say, shouldn't you choose your words more cautiously?"

He stepped back again, cowering in a way before bailing from her chambers.

"How did you fare in the night?" asked Martel.

"All of the incendiary beads were rigged. The task was simple enough thanks to our help. We haven't always been as lucky as to have an inside man like Reeve," replied Opalla.

The two of them walked side by side through the castle gardens, the one place they knew no one would overhear their conversation.

"And you are confident that we haven't aroused any suspicion?" he asked.

"None. Muskus and the other engineers have not once decided to inspect the pipes. I expected more intuition from that man, considering how much he likes to talk about himself," she said.

"He lacks divination for sure, but his mind is rather great," Martel corrected. He had spent much of his time in Darchem with Muskus.

"Disinterested," she blurted. "I received word last

night. The assassination will be committed on the night of the Princess's name day," she said. She looked uncomfortable.

"I know, Reeve informed me. He doubts you," said Martel.

"He confided in you?" she said.

"He is like you, very observant. He spots things other people don't. Now I suspect his suspicion to be misplaced. I have worked with you for eleven years, but I have to ask, my life depends on it," he said.

"You asked, now don't ask again," she said, stern. "On that night, I will feast with the rest of them. I will monitor the guards and the King. You will be in sewers. You will ignite the explosives. There is no escape however from the tower. I've been assessing it for a week."

"I'm not here for suicide, Opalla. Use your great mind. Find another way." He seemed discouraged.

"I will. We still have time. Worry not," she said. As she spoke, she snapped her head to the bushes that engulfed them. "Come out, child."

Aphrayer sheepishly revealed herself.

"I didn't mean to eavesdrop, and I wasn't even listening. I was hiding," said Aphrayer, her words sincere.

"Leave us," Opalla ordered.

Martel bowed and walked back through the gardens and up into the castle.

"You don't listen, do you, girl."

"I swear it, I tried to stay away. I had a bad morning. The cool air helps me calm down. But I heard guards. My mother must have sent them to find me. I only wanted stay out a bit longer, so I hid," she said.

"Have you eaten?" Opalla asked.

"My mother gave the leftovers from breakfast to the hounds. It seems to amuse her," she replied.

"Follow me, learn something." Opalla guided her out of the hedges and bushes and then pointed to a cluster of distant trees. "Every three months, oranges and apples will drop from those two trees. They won't fill you, but they will make you strong. See these bushes, the berries, the purple ones, not the red but the purple. You can eat those. Knowledge is power, use it. You can make a pretty good breakfast from these when the seasons hit. But for now, take this." Opalla reached into her robe and unwrapped a crust of bread.

"You brought this for me?" asked Aphrayer.

Opalla began to fidget, anxiety and worry on her face. "I knew I would stumble into you," she said after a long silence. She then dropped to her knees and grabbed the Princess's hands tightly. "You listen now, as what I am about to tell you won't make much sense at all. On your name day, when your father begins to speak, you make an excuse to use the privy and you run."

"Run, run where? Why? No, I have to deliver a speech after him. I fear that more than my mother's wrath. But my father will anger if I refuse," said Aphrayer, almost making herself cry at the thought.

"You run. You leave. Go to the privy, then head out to these gardens, go deep, further than we are right now.

Head to the gate," advised Opalla as she looked in every direction, hunting for unwelcome ears.

"You're going to take me with you?" Aphrayer steadied her panic.

"I am, but you must be on time, not a second before your father speaks. It has to be timed to perfection, once your father starts talking, he won't stop to address you, and the Queen won't press you too hard as she won't want to arouse suspicion to your suitors' fathers," she said. "Say I understand."

"Aphrayer!" roared a witching voice. "I've had half of your father's guard out looking for you. How many times must you be told, you selfish, stupid girl. You would risk your father's health by leaving him unguarded." The Queen paced across the path and onto the grass, snatching Aphrayer from Opalla.

"The Princess was in the garden, your grace. Our paths meeting is a coincidence," said Opalla.

"You were warned, were you not? I don't like you and I don't trust you either. My husband will hear of it. In the meantime, to the cells. Guards!" screeched the Queen.

Three red cloaks bounded over, delicately passing the Queen before pummelling Opalla down and dragging her away, the pleads from Aphrayer growing more distant.

The cold stabbed at Opalla's dry skin as it snatched her from slumber yet again. She rolled over on the sharp stone floor and chattered her teeth as she tried frantically to warm herself up. A week had passed and, in that time, she had survived on vials of water and harsh rations. Her skin and lips had turned blue, and her body oozed a foul stench.

She sat upright and brushed herself up against the wall, her mind still fixated on the safety of the Princess. She continued to fidget and rummage around the cell, searching and assessing all the weak points of the cell, and the same as yesterday and the day before, she found nothing. In all her years of criminal activity, she had found herself locked up only once before, and she was in captivity a total of twelve hours before she escaped. But these cells were different.

"You don't miss much, do you?" asked a shadow. She turned slowly to the corner of the cell house where a dark shadow sat on a stool, his breath visible now that she was aware.

"You remind me of my right hand, his name is Lumon."

"My King," she greeted, bowing.

"You can identify me in the dark? Impressive," he replied as he stood, approaching the cell's cage.

"I know Martel's voice well enough, and the only other person who would have meaning to come see me would be the King. The Queen probably hopes for you to kill me. For whatever reason however, I do not know," she said.

"You're smart. The whole speech you gave in the throne room that day was comical and the work, the invention, well, truly impressive. Most of my advisors and commanders believe you to be a witch. Women can't possibly be capable of such wonders. No, not in this world," he explained.

"And do you believe that?" she asked as she inspected him. No armour, no blade, she thought. He is not here to kill me, then what does he want?'

"I believe women are much more valuable than men in a way. They have more than one use. My realm would benefit greatly from your mind, your knowledge. For knowledge is power," he said.

"Men usually believe that power is power. Knowledge is irrelevant if you can swing a sword," she said.

"I'm King for a reason. Because of my knowledge and how I use it, Opalla." He began pacing with his hands clasped firmly behind his back. "My wife, the gracious Queen believes you to be mischievous. She claims to have found you snooping, and engaging in conversation with my daughter, my heir."

"I strolled the halls and yes, I spoke with the Princess. I would be flogged, would I not, if I showed ignorance to the Princess. My mistreatment has done nothing but sway me from my work. The deadline you set is now at risk, and without a single visit from Martel, I cannot be sure whether the work has been completed," she said.

"My wife is a strange woman, a hard woman to control. She warms my bed but nothing more, our marriage was a tactical conjoining of houses. Her words ache my ears. I will have you released at once. Confer with your apprentice. He reported to me this morning. It was the first I had heard that you were being detained. He claimed that the sewers were being re-filled and the ladders detached. He seems to have finished the work in your absence," the King said as he took his leave. "You will be released shortly. It's my daughter's name day tomorrow evening. I want you to attend."

Opalla had bathed twice to get rid of the stench and dirt from her week in the black cells. She had dismissed the hand maids and the servants tonight. She wanted to prepare herself for the Princess's party alone. She tied her hair into short plaits and knotted the ends with a bow that held it all back tightly. She then dried her body and put on a tight pair of breeches that covered her down to her shins. She fitted her vest next, two sharp hooked blades strapped to the leather. She put on her flat shoes and to cover all her intentions, she put on a silky blood red dress. A dress fit for a royal ball. Once ready, she stood before the mirror, glaring at herself for a short while, until the door rattled.

"I am to escort you," Officer Apex growled. She withheld a reply and simply opened her chamber door and brushed past him. Martel was not here to meet them this time. She had met with him earlier that morning and given him assignment. He was in position.

She noticed the castle's atmosphere to be a little more

pleasant this evening. Coloured sigils of the various houses that would be present draped the walls, the fire pits and braziers had been set up, battling away the cold, and servants and maids had been positioned at every corner holding trays of silver with foods and drinks of all colours.

"Welcome all, feast, drink, mingle if you will," one of the High King's spokesmen said from a high podium. He repeated his statement as more people flurried into the hall.

The hall was a great square space with a high ceiling in the centre. At the hall's border ran little walkways that were separated by columns and pillars of stone.

Good, plenty of cover, Opalla considered as she took a drink of Zenthian wine for appearance purposes only and walked into one of the walkways. The tables in the central open space were crammed with drunken nobles and a few serious lords who had brought their teenage sons as offerings. She watched them all, figuring out who could potentially be a problem. But thanks to the constant flow of wine and ale, none of them would be able to stand within the hour.

She breezed cautiously between the pillars and lapped the hall twice, figuring out which would be the greatest chance of escape until she calculated the eastern route to be the worthiest. The halls were the least guarded and they led straight for the foyer doors. Once out, she could blend with the shadows and ease her way out to the gate, pick up Aphrayer and then death could claim its prize.

All Opalla had to do now was wait for the High King to deliver his speech. Thanks to the drains and pipes that had been slotted beneath the hall, Martel would be able to hear everything. As soon as The High King got halfway through his speech, he would ignite the explosives, then Opalla had to simply wait for Aphrayer to leave, meet up with Martel, exit the castle and regroup.

"May I have your attention," sounded the King. He was dressed in a dark tunic, silver chains caressing his torso, his golden crown gracing his head. "Today is my daughter's eleventh name day." The crowd roared and cheered her name. "I would like to use this ceremony to give our families a chance to grow ever closer. Some of you lords have spilled blood for me, some of you have fought hand in hand beside me, and some of you have even fought against me. But all of that is the past and we must look to the future! Our children are the future! One lord sitting here in this very hall will have the honour of betrothing his son to my daughter."

Opalla tried to catch the attention of the Princess to remind her of her task, her only task. But instead she captured the fierce eyes of the Queen. She smiled wide, dipping her eyes, almost laughing at her in silence. Next Aphrayer turned to Opalla and confirmed her concern with a simple shake of the head and a wandering tear.

Opalla turned as discreetly as she could, trying desperately not to draw attention, but the second she shifted, the High King snapped his gaze to her, a look of disappointment staining his face as he continued with his speech. She left down the western hall instead of the eastern hall and made for the steps. They descended into darkness, into the tunnels where she found Martel, a flaming torch within his grasp. He leant down and waved the torch over the single pipe that stuck out from concrete and stone.

"Stop!" she yelled.

Martel turned, startled. "What are you doing? You're meant to be keeping up appearances at the hall?"

She approached him slowly, causing him to step back with a look of confusion.

"Put down the torch, we are aborting the mission," she said.

"Reeve was right," he said, furious. "You have gone soft for the Princess, haven't you? Well, you will thank me for it. I won't let you ruin our reputation for some royal squirt who will one day be responsible for the deaths of our people."

"She is innocent, Martel. They were all innocent, all of them. I see the faces of the people we have killed, for what? For coin? For King Artaxes? He is more murderous than the King we seek to kill on this night," she groaned.

"No one is truly innocent, I won't let you do this," he said. He turned and raised the torch to the pipe, before a blade whistled through the air, ripping the flesh from his arm.

He dropped the torch and stumbled back, looking at her in astonishment. Then, in one quick movement, he reached under his robe and drew a silver blade. Opalla drew her other dagger and leaped towards him, slashing at his knee, before spinning back under his swing and cutting at his waist.

Martel yelled out and slammed down with his blade. She crouched and parried the attack with her dagger, holding his sword at bay, but he was stronger and eventually, after a struggle his blade pushed her own down into her shoulder. Martel then angled and pushed down harder, the steel ripping deeper and deeper into her flesh.

Opalla pushed up with all her strength, gave herself an opening and chopped again at his knee. Martel yelled in pain before punching her hard in the face and then picking her up above his head. He launched her at the wall.

The blow winded her but she somehow rolled between his legs, climbed up his back and unleashed hell. She stabbed like a crazed witch, chopping flesh from his back, splitting bone and drawing blood from every new hole that she punctured.

Bloody, bruised and wounded, Opalla stood victorious, yet pride and relief was absent her expression.

"What have I done," she muttered to herself.

She looked down to her dress, thankfully it was red already, so it disguised much of the blood. She sheathed her two blades, rubbed down the blood from her nose and took a deep breath.

She raced up the steps and moved quickly through the western wing and back into the main hall. She placed her arms by her sides, covering the larger patches of blood.

With a quick glance, she flicked her eyes to the royal table as she passed, and to her delight, the Princess was absent. The King spoke with a High Lord whilst the Queen swirled the wine in her goblet.

To the gate then, she thought.

No suspicion, as always. She had once again escaped without consequence. Artaxes would be furious, but Opalla didn't fight for him, she fought for Victor Stran and Victor would protect her like he always had.

She left the hall, passing through the giant black doors and down the eastern hallway.

"Stop!" ordered Lumon. The King's right hand.

A man armoured in black plate with a red cloak draping his back and a golden eagle imprinted on his chest plate appeared before her. Three more warriors were behind him, all with the same armour, except their eagles were silver, not gold.

The huge doors behind her slammed shut. Four more warriors approached.

"No words this time?" Lumon said. "But you've been so clever with them so far. You even cheated the mind of the King. I've not met many people capable of that. No matter, luckily that's what I'm here for. I must admit, this was a close attempt. You really did come close. You might have even succeeded in blowing this place sky high if you hadn't revealed yourself to the Queen. After she grew suspicious, everything seemed obvious from that point. Rig the castle for your so-called invention, rig it with explosives and then boom. It's a shame you have to die, I would have liked to have plucked that brain of yours." He drew his sword and pointed it towards her.

"I served this realm once. I will never serve it again. Victor Stran is my King. Yours will fall before his time, not by me, but someone will end his reign," she spat.

"Perhaps," Lumon grinned and then gave the command.

Anthony Buxton became an author at the age of 22, writing his series The Lost Sons of the West. Anthony also runs a new, modern blog where he shares stories of his personal life, as well as in-depth information about his book series and his plans for the future.

Check out his blog at: anthonybuxtondotblog.wordpress.com

Also by A.L. Buxton

The Lost Sons of the West (Book One)
The Sands Beyond the 7th (Lost Sons of the West Book Two)

Find out more at www.6e.net/albuxton

FUNGAL ROCK

C. K. ROEBUCK

The silence on the stasis deck was broken by the loud shriek of sirens, followed by an intense brightness as overhead lights blinked on. The change from absolute darkness to light would have been enough to send anyone into shock if anyone had been conscious to observe it. Three of the stasis capsules suddenly came to life with a hiss, the freezing gas inside expelled, replaced by heated air, the occupants electro-shocked to life.

Peter awoke, shivering. The warm air around him had not yet permeated his recently frozen body. "Bloody hell," he murmured through chattering teeth. His capsule cracked open, the hydraulic lid lifting to release the warm air to the rest of the deck. He climbed out slowly, dizzy and not yet at full strength after coming out of stasis. He reached down to a drawer in the bottom of the capsule, pulled out his vacuum packed clothes and got dressed as fast as his body would allow.

"Is anyone else up yet?" Peter heard someone shout from the vast depths of the stasis deck.

"Yeah me!" replied another voice from elsewhere.

"Over here, guys," Peter shouted. He recognised the

voices and expected to be hearing them. He was the ship's chief engineer and so Sandra and Jake both worked under him. The moment he awoke from stasis and heard the alarms, he knew the ship must have suffered an engineering malfunction. It was pre-programmed into the ship that any engineering fault would automatically bring these three engineers from stasis so that they could fix the problem.

Peter rubbed his legs to coax more warm blood into them before unsteadily making his way over to a remote computer station. He heard the stumbling footsteps from one of his engineers come into earshot behind him as he started tapping commands on the console.

"What's the news, boss?" asked Jake. "Please don't say I got to get out and push cos it's takin everything I got just to walk."

"Let's hope it doesn't come to that," Peter replied. "I can't access the engineering log from here so I can't tell you what's wrong except that we've stopped accelerating and that shouldn't happen for at least another twenty years."

"Oh well, at least we're still going forwards," Jake stated. "Last thing we need is to have an engine malfunction after we've flipped around to slow down, then end up overshooting the target."

"You're not wrong, but every second we're not accelerating means extra months or years added to our flight time and more time for something to fail," said Peter.

"We had best get cracking then, hadn't we?" said Sandra as she hobbled around a corner into view. "I have a dream to get back to."

They knew she was joking, no one had dreams in stasis.

"So, what do you need us to do, boss?" Jake asked Peter.

"Jake, you go and check the reactor. Sandra, you check the main drive. I'll go to engineering and check the log, see what I can do from there," said Peter.

"Sure thing, boss," said Jake and loped off as fast as his recently defrosted limbs would allow.

"I'll get to that drive," said Sandra. "Keep in touch, yeah! It's a big ship and I'd hate for something to happen to one of us and no one know about it."

"What could possibly happen?" asked Peter. The moment he said the words, he regretted it. If there was one sure way to jinx them and have something bad happen, it was by asking that question.

"You had to say it, didn't you?" Sandra replied in mock disgust.

"Sorry, Sandra. I'll have to be extra careful now," he said laughing.

Moments later, doors were heard opening and closing in distant parts of the deck. Peter performed one last check and closed down the remote station. The corridors of this ship, the Phoenix, hadn't been occupied for over thirty years. From leaving Earth with the remains of humanity held in suspended animation, it had accelerated steadily and not a soul had stirred until now.

The pound of boots on the deck plates were the only

sound in the corridor as Peter made his way towards engineering, then a scratching noise and patter of tiny feet emanated from a nearby air vent. Peter jumped in shock at the sudden break in the otherwise absolute silence.

"Sandra, Jake, I think I just heard rats in the air ducts," he said into his comms.

"Don't be frickin stupid, boss. No heat or food. No way, mate," replied Jake.

"Yeah, what he said. No way, you must be hearing things," added Sandra, laughing.

"Laugh all you want, I know what I heard, guys." Peter shook his head. He knew it sounded crazy, but what else could it be? "Well, just don't come crying to me when they come after you. Let me know if you hear anything weird, okay?"

"Yeah, yeah," mocked Sandra. "Let's just get this boat moving again. I want to go back to sleep."

"You do know we are moving, don't yer?" Jake asked.

"Sure, just not as fast as we should be," came Sandra's reply.

Peter continued his walk, tuned out his subordinates' rabble that came over the comms while subconsciously listening for scratches and squeaks. He didn't hear any more rat-like sounds. There was only the sound of his boots hitting the bare metal floor.

Ordinarily there should be a vibration in the deck plates, a low frequency drone caused by the ion-fusion drive but when Peter put his hand on the cold metal wall of the corridor, he didn't feel any vibration at all.

A shiver ran through him as he thought of the cold stillness, the feeling of being in a huge metal coffin, a ghost ship. So caught up in his thoughts as he was, he missed the turn that was meant to take him to engineering and meandered right into the archive room. In this room, not only was there a record of every earth lifeform, but it was also where the nanites were stored, billions of microscopic robots that would enable them to recreate any creature or plant from Earth when they reached their destination.

Peter immediately realised he had overshot his last turn and backpedalled the way he came, making sure to take the right turn this time. Engineering was the closest destination to the stasis deck and if it hadn't been for missing the turn, Peter would have been the first to arrive, but instead Jake was first to report.

"Hey boss, I'm at reactor control. The reactor looks to be working but it's running in low power mode," Jake announced over the com.

"Any sign of why that is, Jake?" the chief engineer asked.

"Nope, it's as though the fuel tanks are low, but all readings say that's not the case," Jake answered.

"Well, I guess the problem ain't with the main drive then. huh?" put in Sandra. "I'm almost there so I may as well go the rest of the way and check the drive anyway."

"Okay, let me know what you find. I'm looking through the logs now so hopefully I'll find the problem in here," Peter said, lying. He did not want to admit that he, the chief engineer, had made a wrong turn on the ship that he oversaw.

He arrived in engineering, a plain room with three identical computer stations. All the ship's main relay and power conduits were routed behind its walls, ceiling and under the floor. It was constructed so that every panel could be removed, allowing access to the conduits behind.

Peter wiped the thin layer of dust from the console with his shirt sleeve. Sensing pressure on its touch screen, the computer came to life and awaited his input. The engineer tapped in the required commands that brought up the error log but the only error he found relating to the drive was when it shut down after an unexplained drop in power from the reactor. He already knew there was sufficient fuel, and that the reactor was functioning normally, there was only one more thing that could cause the power to drop. The reactor was not solely reliant on the fuel that they brought from Earth. That would consume far too much space onboard the ship which would increase the mass of the ship and in turn create a need for more fuel to propel it forwards. What the reactor did was supplement its fuel with interstellar hydrogen that it collected via a large ram scoop collector on the front of the hull. The reactor would use the captured and modified fuel along with the onboard deuterium to fuel a reaction that would power the ship systems and fuel the main drive.

Peter found the problem further back in the log. The fuel collected by the ram scoop had ceased and as a result, the reactor had shut down to minimum so as not to use all the onboard fuel, which it would need later to slow down. What he had to do was find out why the fuel wasn't getting through from the ram scoop. The sensors on the ship's bow were showing that it existed, and they were not in a void, yet for some reason it was not getting the fuel where it needed to go.

The comms clicked to life. "Hey guys, I'm at the main drive and other than the fact that it is shut down, I can't find anything wrong with it," announced Sandra.

"That's okay, Sandra. It's pretty much what I expected," answered Peter. "I've done checking the logs, and it looks like there's a problem with the fuel not getting from the ram scoop to the reactor."

"Could it be the converter, mate?" Jake asked him.

Peter had already ruled that out. "Sorry Jake, I wish it was that easy but no, the log shows that the converter is fine. It just stopped receiving anything to convert."

"We're going to have to physically check the pipes, aren't we?" said Jake. It wasn't a question. "I told em it was a mistake to skimp on sensors but oh no, why do we need to put sensors in a pipe that are exposed to the vacuum of space they said," he added, sounding angry.

"Okay, Jake. You can tell them you told them so when we get to Tau-Ceti," scoffed Sandra.

"Yeah, well I will," he shot back.

"Look guys, I agree it would have made sense in hindsight to have sensors everywhere possible, but getting pissed off about it now is not helping. I'm just thankful we have drones onboard for just this kind of purpose."

"Good point, boss, rather them than me. You know those maintenance ducts are not the easiest to crawl through," Jake pointed out.

On the console in front of him, Peter called up the drone remote control screen and activated one of the drones, sending it to the location where the problematic pipe joined the converter. While Peter waited for the drone to reach its target, he decided to make use of the time and access stellar chartography to verify their position. It took longer than he expected for the ship sensors to identify and calculate the distances and positions of the surrounding stars. Peter was beginning to get concerned when the result finally graced the screen in front of him. They were exactly where they were supposed to be, roughly one third of the distance to Tau-Ceti from Earth. A beep sounded to inform the engineer that the drone had arrived at its location and had begun its scan of the pipe.

Peter heard the deck plates ringing from two pairs of boots hitting the floor, coming down the corridor toward him. The sound of the boots on metal mingled with that of voices raised in debate about whether they believed the theory about the asteroid that wiped out the dinosaurs. He turned his head as they entered the room just as movement on the screen caught his eye.

"What the hell!" exclaimed Sandra, knocked backwards by Peter as he jerked and fell back into her.

Jake burst out laughing at the exchange, but neither he nor Sandra had seen what Peter had seen.

"A bit jumpy, ain't yer, boss?" said Jake when he finally managed to stop laughing long enough to take a breath.

Peter turned around. He didn't look amused at Jake's outburst.

"Sorry, boss, but you did look like you'd seen a ghost."

"No, but I definitely saw a rat," he replied, calming down a little from seeing the brown, hairy, long tailed rodent scurry past the drone's camera.

"Impossible," both Jake and Sandra said together, shaking their heads in unison.

Peter tapped some controls on the console, rewound the video and played it back, frame by frame to the point where there could be no mistake at the brown head and evil red eye staring back at them.

"Shit, there goes the impossible, guys," announced Peter before tapping another key to switch back to live view.

"I have a question," said Sandra breaking the silence. "What have they been eating?" she asked warily.

"You wanna go and check our MREs?" asked Peter. "My guess is, they're all gone." He knew they would be all gone, without any other food on board, the emergency ration packs would have made a tasty treat for a pack of rats.

"Sure, I'll go," offered Sandra, despondent. She turned around and walked out into the corridor, her boots scuffing against the deck plates indicating her reluctance to carry out her task.

Jake and Peter continued to watch the live video feed from the drone, both trying to prepare themselves for another bristly encounter. Halfway along the pipe and still no fault found, Peter tapped some keys and sent another drone to check the outside of the ship where the other end of the pipe met the void of space.

The wait was agonising, watching the two video feeds from the drones and expecting to find something not right but having no idea what. The internal drone was almost at the end of its travel down the length of the pipe when it pinged an alert. A huge hole in the pipe became visible and as the drone got closer to investigate, gnaw marks could clearly be seen around the edges, marks unmistakably left by the teeth of rats.

The comms clicked to life unexpectedly causing both Peter and Jake to jump.

"Erm, boss. I've got bad news," said Sandra

"Spit it out, Sandra, the suspense is killing me," replied Peter sardonically. He knew precisely what she was going to say.

"They've cleaned us out boss, not one MRE left," exclaimed Sandra.

Peter couldn't make out if she was more shocked or angry. Sandra wasn't squeamish or easily afraid, but she obviously didn't like it when someone or in this case something stole her food.

Eager to move away from the distraction that he could currently do nothing about, Peter tapped a command to send the internal drone into the pipe, a pipe that should hold nothing of interest to rats and should also have no atmosphere but instead the pipe that was showing positive pressure, not a vacuum. The further along the inside of the pipe that the drone traversed the more matter its sensors detected. It started off with a few rat droppings, gradually increasing in number the further into the pipe the drone travelled.

"What the hell's that?" uttered Peter, jabbing his finger at the display. He tapped the relevant commands, stopping the drone in its tracks.

"What are yer looking at, boss," asked Jake, not noticing at first what the chief engineer had spotted. But then Peter spread his fingers on the display, zooming in on the strange grey substance that was clinging to the inside wall of the pipe.

"Damn, that's not supposed to be there," he said.

"What do yer think it is?" Jake couldn't help saying, knowing full well that Peter was just as clueless as he was.

"I don't know, Jake," Peter tapped a command and the displayed image changed as the drone set off once more along the pipe. "Let's check out the rest of the plumbing and see if there's more of whatever that is."

A few minutes later, the drone sent back an alert. It had picked up movement in the pipe. An automatic anticollision subroutine kicked in, driving the drone to increase its height and halt its forward momentum, its sensors reading the way ahead blocked. On Peter's command, the camera rotated down to see why the drone elevation had increased. There could be no mistake. There, below the drone, were three rats, their maws buried deep in what appeared to be the same grey substance they had seen further back down the pipe. The rats, seemingly oblivious to the drone above, continued their feast undisturbed while Peter had the camera rotate up and zoom in on the obstruction ahead.

The external drone at that moment sent back an alert. It had crested a ridge at the front of the ship. The ridge, part of the ramscoop funnel that fed into the pipe, housed powerful coils and generated a deflector field that was meant to repel pretty much anything except interstellar gases. As the drone's angle changed, the camera titled down the funnel and the video feed changed from the star studded blackness, the same moment that the feed from the internal drone's camera came into focus.

The two images could not be more different, the internal drone was showing a mass of grey that completely filled the pipe, whereas the external drone was showing the smooth metallic funnel of the ramscoop and dead centre, right at its core, sat a reddish ragged rock.

"I guess we know why the rats aren't being sucked out, don't we, boss?" offered Jake smiling.

Peter turned to face him, clearly not amused.

"Sorry boss, defence mechanism," was all he could say.

"That's blown out, not sucked, Jake," corrected Peter. "It's a shame really, we wouldn't have to find a way to get rid of them if they had."

"So, what's the plan, boss? How are we going to dispose of the rats and the space rock?" Jake asked him.

"Let's not forget that grey substance, whatever it is," said Peter. "First we get our drones to take samples of the rock and the grey stuff to see what we are dealing with." Peter tapped more commands on the console, instructing the drones to take the required samples of rock and grey matter. It took a while to obtain the results because the drones did not possess the necessary sensors to accurately identify the contents of the samples, instead the drones had to deposit their extracted materials into a special enclosed diagnosis chamber in the ship's science lab. The process was completely automatic which meant that Peter did not have to bring anyone else out of stasis to help with the problem.

Peter activated his comms. "Sandra, we have some samples going to the diagnosis chamber in the science lab and you're closest. There's no data link from the science lab to engineering so I need you to…" he said.

"You need me to save your little legs, hop along and report the results back to you, how's that?" she asked cutting in.

"Thanks Sandra, you're a gem," said Peter, smiling. After a moment's thought, he turned to Jake. "C'mon, I have an idea," he said. He turned and walked out of the door, heading towards the archive room that he accidentally walked into earlier.

"You do know how to program these things, don't you, Jake?" Peter asked rhetorically. He knew damn well that Jake was trained in many things, one of them being micro robotics, the programming and operating of nanites.

"Really? You want me to kill the rats with nanites," Jake asked when Peter told him what he wanted him to do and surprised that Peter would choose to dispense of the rodents that way. "You do know that we have warfarin on board, don't yer, boss. It's quite an effective rat poison," he suggested.

"Sure I do, but warfarin will just make them a smelly mess and it won't turn them back into the food they stole, will it?" replied Peter, his lip curling up into a vengeful grin.

"I'll get started right away boss," said Jake, his mouth mirroring his superior's.

Peter had nothing to do but watch and keep quiet as Jake tapped away on the console in front of him. He knew that no one knew this system better than Jake, but he also knew that programming these nanites demanded Jake's complete attention. One wrong keystroke and instead of turning rats into semi-tasty food, they could end up with flesh eating acid.

"Okay, done," announced Jake as he hit the last keystroke. "I programmed them to disassemble the rats to their basic molecules and reassemble the particles back into the MRE's on file that we had on board. You do realise that won't make up to the same amount that they ate, don't you?" he asked.

Peter was about to reply 'yes', he did realise that, but before he could utter a word, Sandra walked in holding out a flash drive.

"Here you go, boys, the results," said Sandra, passing the flash drive to Jake. "What did I miss?"

"Oh, nothing much. Peter wants me to turn rats into dinner," joked Jake.

Sandra looked like she might throw up at the thought.

"Well, kind of anyway. I'm going to use the nanites to convert the rats back into the rations that they ate," he added before Sandra could throw up on him.

"Yum, sounds lovely," was her sarcastic reply. "What's for dessert, fungus pie?"

"What?" Peter asked, not sure if she was still being sarcastic because she said it with the utmost sincerity.

"Sorry, didn't I mention that grey stuff… it's a kind of fungus and that rock is covered in it," she said

"Jake, do you think…?" Peter started to ask.

"Yeah, I do," replied Jake on the same wavelength. He pushed the flash drive into a waiting slot and started once more tapping away on the console.

"This is why I have you two come out of stasis with me, this!" Peter said, grinning like a Cheshire cat. As he watched Jake work, a thought came to him. He had forgotten something important. He turned to Sandra. "The rock… what is it made of?" he queried.

"Oh, that's easy," she answered. "On the inside, it's primarily basalt. It's the outside that's interesting."

Peter raised an eyebrow, his interest peaked and eager for her to continue. "Go on," he urged.

"The rock is not just covered in that grey fungus but also polarised metal fragments. I'm assuming that's how it got past the deflector field. And it's also slightly radioactive," she said. "Don't worry though, it's not enough to be dangerous but it could be the warmth its generated that somehow helped the fungus to stay alive in space."

Peter was sceptical about a fungus being able to live in the dark, cold vacuum of space with nothing but the warmth of a radioactive rock to grow from, but he simply could not think of any other viable explanation.

"Yes!" Jake finally answered.

"You've done it?" Peter asked.

"Done what?" asked Sandra, puzzled by the two men's success at communicating, without actually communicating.

"I've programmed the nanites to not only break down the rats' organic structure and reorganise it into something that resembles our ration packs but to do the same to the fungus too," answered Jake proudly

"I'm assuming the nanites won't be taking the reconstituted rations back to the mess where the rats found them?" said Peter, suspecting that it would take far too long for the microscopic robots to move the food that far. The shake of Jake's head confirmed what he already believed. "I'd best program the drones to do that. The moment the fungus and rats are gone from that pipe, I'll have the drones seal it up and extract the rock too."

"Don't you want to check out that rock and find out more about it, like where it came from?" asked Sandra.

"Sorry, no, we have samples. We do our job, fix the plumbing, get the ship back underway and we go back to sleep," answered Peter in a tone that made it clear, his decision was final. "The important thing is, a few laser blasts and that rock should no longer be a problem."

Since it was not guaranteed that all the rats were confined to the area of the pipe, Jake supplied several drones with batches of nanites and a directive to dispense them wherever they found those furry rodents or the fungus.

It wasn't long before the food stores started to fill up with the food. Satisfied that the pipe was clean of all contaminants barring the rock in the end, Peter ordered drones to patch up the pipe where the rats had chewed through and confirm it was sealed. Once more, he sent a drone outside the ship to the rock, only this time instead of taking samples, it blasted the rock with a high powered laser, fracturing the rock enough to loosen it. The millisecond the rock was loose, positive air pressure still inside the pipe did the rest and blasted the rock away into the darkness.

"Here goes, guys," said Peter, tapping the command that would bring all drive and power systems back online. Red indicators on the display began to turn green, starting with output from the converter, power to the reactor and then at last, the main drive engaged and the ship resumed accelerating once more.

Walking back to their stasis pods, Peter stopped, reached out and placed a hand on the wall.

Jake looked at Peter as he just stood there grinning. "Everything ok boss?" Jake asked, confused by this.

"Everything is just as it should be," he said.

Craig is an electronic engineer originally from Barnsley, South Yorkshire, and has lived in County Durham for over twenty years. Craig has been an avid sci-fi fan since watching Blakes 7 and Space 1999 as a child, and since then he has loved both watching and reading sci-fi. Craig took to writing after many years of reading when a couple of friends convinced him to write for Harvey. He is currently working on his first novel, Sleep, of which Fungal Rock is a spin off. Sleep and Fungal Rock are both set in the same fictional universe as Splinter of Hope. Splinter was his debut as a writer and can be found in Harvey Duckman Presents Volume 6.

Craig's blog can be found at blog.cragy.org.uk and he's on Twitter as @CKRoebuck

HELL'S FALLS

LIAM HOGAN

It was at her back, a constant reminder. Nothing Freya could do to forget about it, not even for an instant.

An empty quiver.

Or as *good* as empty. To shoot one's 'last arrow' was a common metaphor, for either retirement or death, and to the army those were pretty much the same state of un-being. She was seasoned enough – a veteran of a half dozen brutal campaigns – not to own the ornamental arrow greener archers superstitiously carried. An arrow that couldn't *ever* be shot, which meant their penultimate arrow was effectively their last, false logic negating everything they were taught. As if fate could be so easily cheated!

She remembered her archery master drumming it into them, a decade and a lifetime ago.

"What is an archer without any arrows?" he had asked, whenever he came across an empty quiver on the practice range.

They had been taught to quit the field of battle *before* that point. To resupply, and then to return. And always to save one last arrow because, though it might be virtually useless in a full battle, it still provided some defence in a skirmish on the fringes. Many an unarmed, retreating archer had been cut down by an opportunistic light calvary raid en route to the supply wagons.

Well, there would be no resupplying for Freya.

She had been caught the wrong side of the ravine when the ancient stone bridge had collapsed. Under the weight of a war elephant, no less, the sound of its final trumpet mingling with the thunder of falling stones and the shriller sound of the unfortunate mahout. There had been an even dozen of them who had made the other side before the collapse, three scouts, a far too eager Captain and his far less eager deputy, three men-at-arms, and four archers.

Too few to do much of anything, too many to effectively hide.

The Captain, a pimpled youth, had of course taken charge of this ragtag group of misfits, despite his obvious lack of experience, despite the fact he knew none of their names, not even that of his deputy. Regroup, was the order of the day. A sensible strategy, except there was a deep ravine that cut through the Arkhan range, the jagged highlands that divided the feuding kingdoms. So, like an ass between piles of hay, they had two choices. The safest fordable point was below the rapids, a half-day's quick march down the sloping path. It would take them another half day to get back to the spot they could still see on the other side, the cloud of rubble and dust having already dissipated. Still, that was the *prudent* option. But where, Freya could almost hear the Captain's thought process as it toyed with their lives, was the glory in that? The battle was sure to be over, them having taken no part in it and having flogged themselves stupid just to arrive in time for its conclusion.

The riskier choice was to head upstream, to the Hell bridge, to follow the original orders, but with only a fraction of the intended numbers. General Blaxley had split his troops, aware that the lack of crossing points created a potential bottleneck. He'd hoped that the distraction of a flanking force just as the main army arrived at the larger bridge would create enough confusion to prevent an outright attack and thus allow them to regroup relatively unscathed.

The splinter of the diversionary force, now stranded on the north side of the ravine, would follow the twisting path that shadowed the river upstream. As indeed would the main bulk of the army, plodding along a similar path on the southern side, their numbers swollen by those who would otherwise have crossed by the old, long neglected bridge.

The difference between the two routes was that the south side belonged to the three Kingdoms. While the north was enemy territory, ruled over with an iron fist by the despotic Emperor Ulfred, the killer of women, the blinder of babies.

Or so they had been told, anyway. The three kingdoms had only recently stopped squabbling among themselves. Perhaps a common foe painted black was the glue they had always needed.

It didn't really matter to Freya. The new conflict kept her in coin, and there weren't that many alternative jobs that didn't involve the common drudgery her mother and sisters had suffered. At least General Blaxley allowed women in his army. Half his archers were female and a fair number of the scouts. There was even a handful of women-at-arms, toughened not only by battle but the constant need to prove themselves among the heckling men.

Freya longed for their capable company, for *anyone* other than this callow, unproven youth of a Captain. Under his command, they never really had a choice at all. At the exposed fork in the path, one heading down and west, the other east, his deputy had urged caution and it was while the Captain was cursing him for a coward and a fool that the enemy patrol had fallen upon them.

If any of the scouts had scattered and survived, she hadn't seen them since. She herself was only alive because she had by then climbed out of earshot, tired of the limited vocabulary of the Captain. Why, she'd shared ales with soldiers whose sweet nothings were more inventive and far more filthy. As she sat basking in the thin sunlight, glad to finally be even briefly away from the thundering noise of the river, to be able to hear herself think, she heard the cries and the sound of clashing metal, the dull *thwonk!* of crossbow bolts being fired.

She had emptied her quiver onto the skirmish below, but it had been a lost cause. The Captain and the other two unarmoured archers, they had been dead even before she shot her first arrow. Roberts, the Captain's deputy, and the men-at-arms had battled valiantly and her aerial assault had evened the odds, until there were only two left, Roberts, and a giant of a foe, swinging his bastard sword to and fro in great arcs.

And, veteran or not, had Freya not fatally paused, reaching for what had turned out to be her last arrow? In that instant, Roberts had snuck inside the giant's guard, even as the sword-and-a-half had come slamming down on his helm. The simultaneous clash of their swords had spelled both their dooms.

For a moment, the ravine fell shockingly silent as Freya mentally cursed her indecision. In all probability, it wouldn't have made any difference. It would have had to be a miracle shot to pierce the giant's armour. Though she'd made such shots before, the metal was often thinner at the rear. Too late to find out.

Too late to descend as well, to gather up what weapons and supplies were strewn across the rocky ground. Even as she was about to start her scramble down, she'd heard the holler of alarm, the approach of enemy reinforcements, and had slipped instead back around the rocky outcrop and out of sight.

The second enemy patrol must have deduced she was there – from the angle of the arrows perhaps – because they'd been on her heels ever since. Perhaps that would have been okay if she had been heading west, towards safety. But she too never had that option. The paths that cut through the rocky formations were few and the only escape from her lofty perch had driven her upstream.

Sooner, if not later, she was bound to run into another patrol and be caught betwixt and between, a single arrow to her name.

She tried, as much as was possible, to avoid the narrow path. There was no cover there, nowhere to hide. Though she was fleeter of foot than her pursuers, they travelled the straighter line, not needing to scramble up or indeed down as the chasm twisted and bucked, leaping from rock to rock.

She'd considered trying to hide long enough that they would pass, allowing her to double back, take the safer route. But how much safer would it really be? And what if, instead of blindly going by, they discovered her? Every time she paused, every time she heard – or thought she heard – their approach, her nerve failed her and on she would push, until yet again she tired, or found some shelf or a cleft that might make an even better hiding place. Perhaps if she could wait until night?

But the sun hadn't even reached its peak. And she had only the one small canteen and a few strips of jerky.

And, as the quiver bouncing uselessly against her back kept reminding her, a single arrow.

Freya had half considered leaving it behind. The arrow, the quiver, even the bow, its awkward length as much a hindrance as anything else, slung over her shoulder its occasional rattle against stone causing her to quietly swear.

Ahead, there was a lingering cloud that spread and

softened the midday sunlight. She'd wondered at that. The mist that had greeted the day's dawn was long burnt off. It was only as she recognised a new sound to the constant background of the turbulent river, echoing in its narrow gorge, that she realised with a quickening of her pulse what it was.

Hell's falls!

She was within spitting distance of the bridge that the General's main force would soon be crossing, if they weren't already there. Spitting distance from safety, or at least safety in numbers.

All she had to do was reach it before her pursuers caught up with her. Reach it without falling foul of anyone else lurking this side of the river. Reach it without – she almost laughed aloud – being mistaken as the enemy from her own side.

Simple enough, she smiled to herself.

Though surely, inevitably, the bridge would be guarded, would it not? She would have to hope that she'd timed it to arrive when it had already been secured by the General. He, in turn, must know his plan to mount a diversion had fallen into the ravine along with the elephant and the remains of the bridge. Would that make him more cautious? To delay approaching the choke point until he was entirely sure of the lay of the enemy?

It seemed it would be a good idea to get a lay of the enemy herself.

Above loomed a high pinnacle of rock, jutting out from the cliff. Seemingly unscalable, but there was a crack that started just ahead. She chewed her lip, considered the matter. Was she becoming careless, with her destination so close? The crack looked easy enough to climb, for someone of her size, her slender frame, but how exposed would it leave her? On the other hand, once she was out of reach of the crossbows, would she cease to be of much interest? Surely no one would be bothered to climb after her, not with the far more important bridge so close by.

If she had a coin and time to let it decide…

She was climbing before the thought had finished playing itself out in her head. Fate! She was never keen to give that cruel mistress the chance to decide her future, never keen to cheat her either. Other soldiers played with dice, or cards, or indeed coins. Other soldiers made bargains with unseen forces or jealously hoarded protective amulets and charms. Not Freya.

As she scaled the rock, there was a nagging doubt each time the going got tough, but when there was an echoing cry from below, the skitter of crossbow bolt against stone, she knew it was too late to change her mind. At least she was out of range.

She was glad she was so lightly equipped when she discovered an overhang, one that hadn't been visible from down below. More encumbered, she might not have been able to scramble up and over it, her fingers, wiry and strong from years of pulling the bowstring, found the small holds she needed to pull herself up.

The rest of the way was easier, and then she was stood

atop the tower of rock. She marvelled at the view, the halo of the spray from the falls directly before her, backlit by the sun. She could see both sides of the ravine, and there! The glint of steel, the sinuous movement of a snaking army. No doubt the General would be near the vanguard. All she had to do was to find somewhere to safely wait and rejoin them.

She scanned their route. The main bulk of the force – including the two remaining war elephants – were about a mile away from the falls and the bridge that spanned them. She could see a couple of scouts, just now approaching the first buttress. And the way ahead for them, the whole bridge, was blissfully clear of opposition.

Immediately after it and on her side of the ravine, not very far away at all, there was a large open space, rare, in this rock-tortured region. The General would be sure to regroup there. And the sheer number in his company would dissuade the patrol that had dogged her flight. As soon as they got wind of the army's arrival – if they had any sense – they'd make themselves scarce, clearing the way for her descent.

She might as well get started now, she thought. Wait at the overhang, safely out of reach of the crossbows, out of sight too, but half the climb back down.

Only, as she turned to do so, she caught another glimpse of sun against bare metal, from an unexpected direction. She crooked her hand over her brow, trying to peer through the shroud.

There! A pair of dark clad men, almost invisible against

the rock. They were at a lower height than her, but above and the other side of the gathering place.

Enemy scouts? To warn of the approaching army?

She kept watching, aware vaguely that across the ravine the General's forces were getting closer. Now she knew what to look for she quickly found a second pair of waiting dark figures on a different outcrop. And a third. Each suspended high above the bridge and the bowl of the gathering place. The hairs on her arm prickled.

What could so few men do, though? Raise the alarm, sure, but the General had never expected to cross unnoticed. Or was it something more cunning?

She thought of the tumbling rock that had stranded her. An attack on the bridge? It had stood for centuries, far larger and stronger than the one that had fallen. Besides, the men were in the wrong place for that. Even if they were to drop a ton of rocks…

Oh.

If the enemy were to employ enough of the infernal black powder that fuelled those new-fangled cannons, if they had identified weaknesses, fractures in the rock face, if they managed to attack those all at the same time, then the gathering place wasn't just a conveniently flat stretch. It was a bowl into which all those rocks would fall. A killing bowl.

She edged to the side of the cliff she was on, and carefully peered over it. As she had suspected, there was yet another half-hidden crew, a little to the left, on a narrow shelf of rock. And this close, she could see the dozen or so small barrels they had wedged into the crevice fifty feet directly below her. She glanced back to the men, saw that one of the hooded figures was holding a smoking brand ready to drop onto spilt black powder. Waiting for the right moment.

It would be a massacre. If any of the General's army survived, they would be in no fit state to fight a war, and if the Emperor Ulfred was this well prepared, then no doubt somewhere just out of range of the falling rocks a force was ready to mop up any stragglers.

She had to warn them!

But how? A shout would not be heard, not over the clamour of the falls. She found herself reaching for her last arrow, carefully nocking her bow. If she pulled the string as far as she could, would the arrow reach the bridge? Maybe. But would a single arrow be enough to stop the approaching force, to tell them of the threat ahead?

She shook her head. Unlikely, and the downdraught from the falls was just as likely to make her miss. She could wait until they began to gather on her side, that was definitely within her range especially at this elevation, but might that already be too late?

And if the pair of men lurking below her exploded their cache of gunpowder, what would remain of the splinter of rock she was on? Would it still stand? Or, split by the fracture she had climbed, would the whole giant edifice slip lazily forward, taking her with it?

Ah damn it!

The two scouts were crossing the bridge now, fanning out into the gathering place. The enemy above them was too well concealed from that angle. A wave of a bright strip of cloth – the all clear.

Below, she watched the hooded man stretch out his arm, the one containing the smoking brand, awaiting their own signal to action.

She closed her eyes. Accursed fate! There was only one certain way to stop this. She took careful aim. He was a sitting duck, but she wanted to make sure that when he fell, he fell the right way. She watched him, kissing the fletch of her last arrow, as the second man, a little higher and with a view over the bridge, held out his fist – get ready.

She never had to overthink her shots. The arrow leapt from her fingers with barely a conscious thought, triggered by some subtle shift in the man's position.

There was a muffled *ugh!*, and then he pitched slowly forward, as she knew he would, still clutching the brand.

As he fell the short distance, spinning silently like a leaf, she wondered idly if all the other caches around the bowl would take it as a signal to trigger their own explosions.

But it didn't much matter.

One would do it.

Liam Hogan is an award-winning short story writer, with stories in Best of British Science Fiction and in Best of British Fantasy (NewCon Press). He's been published by Analog, Daily Science Fiction, and Flame Tree Press, among others. He helps host Liars' League London, volunteers at the creative writing charity Ministry of Stories, and lives and avoids work in London. More details at happyendingnotguaranteed.blogspot.co.uk

THE EAGLE'S FLIGHT

KATE BRUCHEREL

The crowd at the gates showed no sign of dissipating. Finch stood on the hostel balcony with half a dozen other young travellers and gazed morosely down at the sea of beings clamouring for access to the park. They had been here on Ersyn for three days, waiting in vain for the legendary water park to re-open after some unscheduled maintenance downtime.

"Do you reckon we'll get in?" asked a squat Venusian troll.

"I hope so," replied Finch. "I don't think those gates are opening any time soon, though."

The troll grunted and turned away from the balcony railings. "I give up," he said. "I'm shipping out to Cygnus tomorrow. There's no way I'd get to ride the flumes now with so many people ahead of me."

"You're going straight to Cygnus?" asked Finch. "I've taken the longer tour. My next transit's in two days."

"I still don't fancy your chances of getting in," said the troll. "Ah well. Enjoy the rest of your trip, Finch."

"Thanks," said Finch, "you too. Maybe catch up with you further along the tour?"

"Maybe." The troll waved as he disappeared back into the hostel.

They would probably not cross paths again, reflected Finch. The round-the-galaxy tour itineraries were very flexible. It was a centuries old tradition among avians like Finch to set out on a journey as unformed youngsters and return as gendered adults, ready to take on their responsibilities in the clan. They tended to take their time, savouring the rite of passage. Venusian trolls, apparently, were a hastier race, catching the main sights before rushing back to the hot gravity well of the Sol system that they called home.

Finch looked back at the crowds, the closed gate, and the high walls. There was a tantalising glimpse in the background of the empty water park. There would be no amount of teasing back home if Finch missed visiting this landmark. Ersyn was a fast-spinning planetoid, its high centrifugal force one of the factors which made the water park so popular. The two days left before departure amounted to a little less than twenty-eight standard galactic hours. It was already after noon. If the gates were to open now, there would still be little chance of reaching the front of the queue until late the next day. That was cutting it very fine indeed.

Finch leaned over the balcony, trying to get a better look at the interior of the park. The sun was starting to cast shadows on the smooth surfaces, and as Finch watched, it became clear that there was a lot of frantic activity behind the scenes. There was no one in direct sight, but the shadow play revealed people moving around and many agitated limbs waving. There was obviously something very wrong with the legendary flumes.

Finch's eyes rose to the top of the ride which dominated the skyline.

The Eagle's Flight.

This was the crowning glory of the galaxy's water parks. Sharing a picture from the top of that chute would be enough of a brag to keep the family quiet. How hard could it be?

Scanning the high walls of the park from the balcony's vantage point, Finch noticed a spot where the tourist crowd thinned out and the perimeter ran close to the network of smaller streets behind the strip. There were trailers obscuring the view, but it looked very much as if this was the trade entrance, hidden from eyes on the ground.

Mind made up, Finch turned away from the railings and headed back inside the hostel and down the stairs to street level. Pausing for a moment to re-orient, Finch struck out through the narrow streets, grateful for the logical grid pattern of the settlement. In the bigger towns on old established planets, especially those with a hive or warren culture, urban layouts were so complex that travellers could be lost for days. As it was, Finch reached the hidden gate in less than quarter of an hour.

For all the activity inside, the gateway was quiet. Only the trailers parked tight against the wall hinted at the work going on. In the jumble of logos, Finch picked out the universal signs for joiners, plumbers, electricians, and what looked oddly like the symbol for fishmongers but probably meant something quite different. There was no security detail at the entrance and the portal was wide open. A couple of sturdy figures emerged, causing Finch to draw back into the shadows. They chatted and joked as they unloaded a large crate from one of the nearby trailers and carried it back through the gate without breaking step.

"This is my chance," murmured Finch. Staying close to the buildings for as long as possible, dusty feathers camouflaged in the shadows, Finch crept towards the gate. There was no movement from within. It was now or never.

Turning the corner into the park, trying to look confident and relaxed, Finch was brought up short by the glorious vista of flumes and rides soaring to the sky. And there it was in the middle, breath-taking and terrifying. The Eagle's Flight.

Caught up in wonder, Finch paused a moment too long.

"Impressive, isn't it," said a voice. The spherical security drone was level with Finch's head. It turned its single eye towards the avian. "I don't think you should be in here, should you, youngster?"

Finch's feathers drooped.

"Follow me," said the drone, sailing back towards the gate.

Finch knew better than to argue. Plan A hadn't worked. There was always Plan B.

The bunk room was empty. The Venusian troll's bed was tidy, and his rucksack gone. Finch took advantage of the peace and quiet to clean and preen, tweaking and smoothing their iridescent black feathers. This second assault on the park required a little more preparation. The security drones would be looking for backpackers and young travellers, not mature workers. As an avian, adding a splash of colour was one way to look more grown up. Finch's feathers were still all black with no sign of a moult hue, the colour that would announce their adult gender. They weren't ready to settle yet.

A little impromptu shopping on the way back to the hostel had yielded a bright blue feather boa and matching satchel. Finch carefully stripped the feathers from the boa and weaved them into their own plumage, adding a noticeable haze of blue which would mark them out as a maturing female. The satchel emphasised the impression. Looking in the mirror, Finch saw a tall, elegant, working avian. Perfect.

The late afternoon sun was casting much longer shadows as Finch left the hostel in search of the right bar. The long strip of bars and restaurants would be full of tourists, but there were plenty of establishments in the side streets which were frequented by locals and by members of the diverse itinerant workforce here on Ersyn.

The first bar, a small bodega with a few barrels for tables, was virtually deserted. The cocktail menu was good and priced for the locals. Finch ordered the best drink in the house and sat at the bar, sipping it happily. This undercover plan was going well.

"Are you working in town, Ma'am?" asked the bartender, polishing a glass absentmindedly on its fur.

Finch tried not to wince at the gendering. At least the disguise was working.

"I'm here for a few days," said Finch cautiously. "Is it usually this quiet in here?"

"It's still early," replied the bartender. "Once the tourists give up trying to get into the water park, this place will be jumping."

"What's the problem with the park?" asked Finch.

"Not too sure what's wrong this time," said the bartender. "It's all a bit fishy if you ask me."

"Do they need any hands?"

The bartender looked Finch up and down. "The trade guilds are always hiring," he said at last. "Try the Omega Lounge on Seventeenth. That's where they hang out."

"Thanks." Finch drained the drink and scanned the payment chit.

"Head east out of here and take the third left," said the bartender. "You can't miss it."

Standing outside the Omega Lounge a few minutes later, Finch had to admit that the bartender was right. The front of the building was a riot of lights and colour. It looked out of place in these back streets away from the strip. Finch took a deep breath and stepped through the door.

Inside, it was busy but much quieter than the exterior

suggested. The music was low and soothing. The clientele seemed to be made up exclusively of workers and locals clustered in groups around large tables. The scent of food wafting through the room made Finch's stomach growl. It smelled good. The odd fourteen-hour day/night cycle meant that most visitors skipped lunch. Slipping into a free space at the edge of one of the tables, Finch looked around for a menu.

A waiter appeared.

"What'll it be, Ma'am?"

"What's on the menu?" asked Finch.

"Today we have fish, potatoes and salad," replied the waiter.

Finch frowned. "Uh… what kind of fish?"

"Fish, potatoes and salad."

Finch looked down the length of the table. Everyone was tucking into the same dish.

"I guess… one fish, potatoes and salad, please."

The waiter nodded. "Beer or aquavit?"

"Beer, please," said Finch. It wouldn't do to start on the local firewater this early.

The waiter disappeared as smoothly as he had arrived and returned in minutes with a glorious plate of food and a huge glass of frothy beer. If nothing else, reflected Finch, savouring the flavours, this was the best meal of the trip so far.

"We don't see many avians in here," said an octopod sitting opposite. She reached out a tentacle in greeting. "I'm Chahidi."

"Finch," said Finch through a mouthful of salad. "Nice to meet you."

"You're plumbing guild too?" asked Chahidi.

"Yes," said Finch confidently. "Are you working on the park?"

Chahidi rolled her eyes. "Are we ever. We're straight back on shift after dinner." She looked Finch up and down. "We could do with an extra tentacle. Wing. Whatever."

"I don't have any experience with flumes," said Finch quickly, torn between elation that Plan B might be working and terror that they would be exposed very quickly as knowing nothing at all about plumbing. "Apart from riding them, of course."

"I like your style," said Chahidi, skin glowing an amused pink. "You can help me out. I'll clear it with the boss." She picked up her glass of aquavit and raised it to Finch. "Welcome to the team."

"Thanks," said Finch sincerely. This was easier than expected. "The fish is good, isn't it?"

Chahidi laughed. "It's excellent. You can tell it's local. Nice and fresh."

"Are there fish farms nearby?" asked Finch. They were in the middle of what passed for a continent on Ersyn, a long way from the sea.

"Kind of," said Chahidi with a smirk. She carried on eating.

Sated and rested, the cheery group of plumbers made their way from the bar to the gate from which Finch had been summarily ejected a few hours before. There was no sign of the security drone as they made their way deep into the park, taking shortcuts through the workings of the rides. Finch gazed around in awe, trying not to gawp like a tourist but fascinated by the spaghetti of pipes which soared to the heights.

"It's usually so loud in here that you can't hear yourself think," said Chahidi. "When we get it fixed, you'll see what I mean."

"Chahidi," called the supervisor, "you and the bird head up to the top gantry."

"Right, boss," replied the octopod happily. "Come on, Finch. Have you got your spanners?"

Finch patted the blue bag confidently. "All set."

Chahidi started expertly up the stairs, tentacles whirling as she pulled herself up by the stair rail and adjacent pipes. Finch tried to keep up and realised that the spin of the planet was providing a little boost to every step and jump. As they rose higher up the structure, Finch looked down. The rest of the plumbers were mere specks on the ground and the top gantry was still some way away, but Finch still had plenty of energy.

"This is fun!"

The octopod turned her head and glowed. "It is, isn't it? Not far now."

The high gantry came into view. A mass of pipes converged at that point, and a grimy window gave Finch a glimpse of the outside world. They were very high up.

"Chahidi…" Finch peered out of the window, trying

to fix on a familiar landmark. "Are we actually inside the Eagle's Flight?"

"Of course we are. Hadn't you worked that out?" Chahidi dumped a large bag of spanners and spares onto the gantry. "Look sharp, Finch. Now that all the blockages are cleared, they're testing the pressure lower down. If all goes well, they'll get the pumps going and open the valves all the way up to us."

"What were the blockages?" asked Finch.

"Haven't you worked that out yet?" said Chahidi. "I guess you're new to the trade. There was a rain of fish four days ago. The little blighters have been all over the park and through the pipes. As soon as a big one gets stuck in a pipe, everything grinds to a halt. This is the best plumbing job in the galaxy. We all watch the weather forecasts, and as soon as they announce fish for Ersyn, every plumber in the nearby systems flies in."

"Fish... No wonder there's so much of it on the menus in town."

"It's taken longer than usual to fix this time. We've been so short staffed. I'm glad you came into the Omega this evening."

"So am I," said Finch, glancing out of the window at the view again and wondering whether there was a chance of getting a picture.

"They never tell the tourists, of course," continued Chahidi. "That's why you signed that confidentiality agreement when you entered your guild…"

She frowned, thinking. Her skin dulled to a grey green. "Which planetary guild are you with, again?"

Luckily for Finch there was a shout from the gantry below.

"Here we go," said Chahidi, doubts forgotten. "I'll start opening the valves. I need you ready." She grabbed two valves with four of her tentacles and pointed at her bag with a fifth. "Grab an M20 and that hammer. If there's a single trickle of water, you need to close that emergency stopcock just there." She pointed across the gantry with a sixth tentacle, tangled herself up in a knot, and collapsed to the floor. "Dammit!"

"Are you okay," said Finch, reaching to help her up.

"Don't mind me," she shouted as the noise began to swell. "Get to those valves, now!"

Finch was tall and had the reach to grab both levers at once but was not strong enough to turn them quickly. Chahidi writhed desperately as the pressure built and the pipe joints threatened to give way.

"Open the one on the left first," she yelled.

Finch concentrated hard and wrestled the left-hand lever to the open position. There was a splashing from outside, and a strange noise came over the roaring of the water. Finch realised it was the crowd cheering outside the gate. Swelling with pride, Finch grabbed the second lever. It was too stiff to move.

"Incoming!" Chahidi, free from the knot, grabbed a can of lubricant and stretched out a tentacle, spraying the mechanism with millimetre-perfect accuracy. The valve opened smoothly.

"Four more," shouted Finch, grabbing the next lever. It was as immovable as the last. "Have you got that spray?"

"I can't help," shouted Chahidi in reply, her voice strained.

Finch turned to look at her. She was stretched across the gantry with a hammer in one tentacle, a spanner in another, the spray clutched in a third, and the rest of her tentacles wrapped tight around groaning joints.

"Get on with it," she yelled desperately. "I can't hold these much longer. It'll blow if the pressure gets too much."

"I can't move the levers," shouted Finch, panicking.

"The last shift was supposed to check them all," she murmured, despairing. The pipes were bulging, and there was no way that the team lower down would be able to shut off in time. There was nothing else for it.

"Catch!"

She threw the can of lubricant in the air. It rose impossibly high before starting to fall. Finch tracked every degree of its parabola and caught it with a triumphant grin.

"Now!" cried Chahidi.

It was the work of moments to loosen the mechanisms and open the remaining valves. The agonising creak of metal gave way to the rushing of water, and a rising crescendo of cheers from the plumbers inside the ride and the crowds at the gate outside.

Finch slid down the wall and sat on the gantry, breathing heavily.

"Teamwork," said Chahidi. "You're a natural, Finch." She cautiously loosened her grip on the pipe joints, one at a time. Colours rippled across her skin as she relaxed. Not a drop of water had been spilled.

The two of them sat in companionable silence for a few moments. "What now?" asked Finch, looking longingly at the door which led from the gantry directly out to the top of the ride, tantalisingly close.

Chahidi looked thoughtful. "I like the way you think." She scrabbled in her bag and pulled out a communicator.

"Boss? Yes, thanks. It was touch and go. The last shift didn't get up here with the lubricant." There were raised voices in the background. "If their bonus made its way to us, that'd be good," said Chahidi quietly.

Finch nodded violently. Some extra travelling money would come in handy.

"Boss? Can we do the final test? Are we cleared to go?"

She crossed her tentacles. Finch could barely breathe.

The communicator crackled into life. "Yes, you've earned it."

"Thanks, boss," said Chahidi. She flung the communicator back in her bag, happy colours swirling around her skin. "We are ready to rock, Finch. Let's ride the Eagle's Flight."

They emerged from the gantry to the top of the ride. Down below, the cheers of the crowd redoubled.

"Wait," said Finch. "We need a picture."

Chahidi grabbed Finch's camera with one tentacle,

caught the startled avian in a tight embrace, and checked that the iconic sign was in shot behind them.

"Smile," she said, quite unnecessarily.

Finch stowed the precious camera in a waterproof pouch in the blue bag and clambered into the rubber raft that would bear them through the greatest flume ride in the galaxy. Chahidi clutched her bag of tools tight with four tentacles and suckered herself to the raft with the other four.

"Ready?"

"Ready."

Cheers ringing in their ears, they launched triumphantly from the top of the Eagle's Flight. The park gates opened, and the crowd flooded in.

A sci fi fan since first seeing the Daleks from behind the sofa, Kate Baucherel works on the application of new and emerging technologies to solve business problems. Sometimes her imagination gets the better of her, and the fictional worlds in her writing are rooted in the possibilities already at our fingertips. Her work includes the SimCavalier futurist cybercrime series, several short stories, and non-fiction books for business leaders.

Search for Kate Baucherel and @SimCavalier on Twitter, Facebook, Instagram, LinkedIn, and Amazon to learn more.

TULLY AND THE ASSASSIN

LIZ TUCKWELL

Tully hated to see the sour-faced visage of Lullius in front of him in the library. That meant Spectacula, the Dowager Empress of Reem, wanted to see him and that was never good. Besides, if she was sending a messenger, he'd rather see her handmaiden Melissa's lovely face. He was, of course, over Melissa now he knew she was one of Spectacula's spies. He just liked to see a pretty girl.

After Spectacula's burly guards granted him admission, Tully entered her chambers. He saw her sitting at her impressive oak desk, scribbling on a tablet. She was silver-haired but still beautiful, with her fine-boned features and large eyes. And one of the most powerful people in Reem.

"Ah, Tully," she said without looking up. People whispered Spectacula had eyes in the back of her head.

"Domina."

Tully stood there rigidly. What awful assignment did she have for him this time?

She looked up. "I've heard worrying rumours that there's going to be an assassination attempt on the emperor." Her network of spies was always busy.

Good luck to them, thought Tully. Timorous was weak and unpleasant. But how did this concern him?

"His body slave's leg was broken yesterday. I want you to find out if it was an accident or deliberate. Start by questioning Grumio."

Tully's shoulders relaxed, and he smiled. For once, it was the pleasant, simple job she was always promising him.

"At once, Domina." He stopped, hand on the door handle.

"Not so fast. What an impatient young man you are."

Tully turned back to face her.

"I also want you to take Grumio's place while he's mending."

Tully stiffened. "But he's a body slave and I'm a scribe," he protested. He wanted to say he had valuable skills and was too good to be a body slave, but he didn't dare.

"I'm sure you can ask Grumio for some tips on how to be a good body slave while you talk to him." It was her turn to smile. "Oh, and Tully, don't forget what happens to slaves whose masters are murdered. Run along now."

Tully shuffled out of the chamber. All slaves in a Reemiard's household were put to death if he was murdered, which said a lot about Reemish masters in Tully's opinion. He'd always thought he'd be safe because he worked in the imperial library. Now his precious security was gone.

"How did you come to break your leg?" Tully asked the sweating slave lying on his pallet in his small, windowless bedroom.

"The emperor asked me to get him a midnight snack and by cursed bad luck some careless fool'd spilt some oil by the entrance to the kitchen and been too lazy to mop it up. I'd got my lamp, but I didn't see it, so arse over tit I went and broke my leg." Grumio gestured at his splinted left leg.

"How terrible," said Tully. "Did you see anybody else around?"

"No. I had to shout and curse myself blue before anyone came to help me."

"Does the emperor often have midnight snacks?"

"Not often."

Spectacula was wrong, Tully decided. This was an accident, surely. Not connected to the assassination rumour she'd heard from her network of spies. He wondered if Grumio had an enemy amongst the household slaves, but who would have known that the emperor's body slave would come hunting for a snack that night?

"The emperor sent his own physician to look at it," Grumio boasted.

"Those Grok physicians are very clever," Tully said.

Not clever enough. Grumio didn't look well to him, wet with sweat and his large face flushed.

"And he asked a priestess of Hekate to give me an amulet. Look!" Grumio jerked up a small lead plaque from around his neck and showed it to Tully.

The inscription read, 'May the gods make this person well as soon as possible. I promise to give three jars of wine if they do so.'

"The emperor will give the gods three jars of wine if you recover? I mean, when you recover?" Tully was impressed. He'd always thought Timorous was a skinflint.

Grumio stopped smiling. "No. He said I'd have to pay for the wine. Even so, he gave me the amulet."

"So, he did," Tully soothed.

"Why are you here?"

"I'm your replacement until you get better. They thought you could give me a few tips."

"Don't break your leg." Grumio scowled.

Tully nodded. "Anything else?" Despite himself, his face fell. Of all the rotten jobs Spectacula had ever forced him to do, this was going to be one of the worst. He could feel it in his water.

"Think you're too good for this?" asked Grumio with a scowl, looking at Tully's downcast face.

Tully did think he was too good to be a body slave. He could speak, read and write Latin, Grok and Koptik, for gods' sake. He belonged in a library, not a lavatory.

"Well, there are perks in being a body slave, you know," Grumio said.

"Such as?"

Grumio levered himself up onto an elbow. "The emperor is very particular. Insists that he only uses a sponge on a stick once when he empties his bowels. Then I put it in a jar, and I have to wash each used one out later."

The Emperor of Reem, who had more territories and money than sense, made his body slave wash out the sponges for his bottom.

"But there's wear and tear, of course. The sponges have to be replaced." He winked. "There's people will pay good money for imperial poo, so they will."

Tully raised a sceptical eyebrow.

"It's true," Grumio insisted. "They think it brings them good luck. I make good money out of selling it. I'll tell you who to deal with if you'll agree to split it fifty fifty."

"Suppose the emperor finds out?" Or worse, his mother, Spectacula. Tully could imagine her reaction. He shuddered.

"Timorous? That twit?" Grumio laughed. "He doesn't know what side of bed to get out of in the morning. He'll never notice. What do you say?"

Tully said no. He'd been tempted, he was never averse to making some more money and his freedom fund wouldn't grow itself. But Spectacula's spies were everywhere. To make up for his refusal, he fetched the slave some wet cloths and another jug of wine before he left. He even emptied his brimming chamber pot.

"I'm lucky. I don't have a sense of smell," Grumio said as he noticed Tully's nose wrinkling.

Tully trudged behind the Emperor Timorous and his sidekicks, laden down with buckets, mops, bags and jars.

As they neared the bathhouse, he noticed a shabby, thin man limp to the shop opposite, lean against the wall and hunch over a tablet. He reminded Tully of someone, but he couldn't think who. Tully switched back to thinking about his unpleasant job. He was scowling as Timorous turned around and beckoned to him. He quickly changed his expression to a servile smile.

"You, whateveryournameis, go in there and give it a good clean," Timorous instructed him. He was as charming as his twin brother, Tremulous, whom Tully knew only too well. Like Tremulous, he could never be bothered to learn the names of new slaves.

Tully put down the bag and pot and trudged into the noisome lavatory, clutching a bucket of water and a mop. He'd hoped they would keep the lavatory in the imperial bathhouse in better order. After all, it was decorated to the highest standard with a skilfully painted mural which showed the gods having a pissing contest. He was wrong. The stench was appalling. Grumio was right, no sense of smell was a godsend in his profession.

"Get on with it!" Timorous shouted from outside. "I need to go!"

So do I, thought Tully, far away from this place. But he was stuck with the emperor for the time being. Spectacula wanted her precious baby boy kept safe. That not only meant twenty-four-hour cover from the Praetorian Guard, but someone keeping an eye on him wherever he went. Including the lavatory.

Tully mopped the lavatory. Whoever had laid a mosaic

floor hadn't thought about the poor slaves trying to keep it clean. He moved on to the top of the stone bench that the bowls were set into, trying not to gag as he did so. As soon as he'd finished, the emperor rushed in, followed by several of his cronies. They hoisted up their tunics, plonked their backsides on the bowls, then gossiped about the recently departed Jyptian delegation.

"Did you see what the ambassador's wife was wearing? Linen so fine you could see her nipples through it."

"Scandalous. No decent Reemish matron would wear such an outfit," the emperor said.

"Only a Reemish whore!"

"Lucky Antonius Turbulous getting sent to Jypt!"

They guffawed and dug each other in the ribs along the line.

"Why didn't the Jyptian queen come?" Senator Publicus Flavius Stultus asked.

"Some paltry excuse. She'd just had a baby."

"And didn't want to get knocked up again so soon by some virile Reemiard?"

They all laughed again.

Tully had met the slaves of the Jyptian delegation. They'd seemed a standoffish lot, couldn't speak Latin, and didn't respond even when he spoke to them in Koptik. That had been a shame. He liked to practise his Koptik as it was getting rusty. Tully started to move outside.

"Where do you think you're going?" Timorous asked, frowning at him.

"To get the sponges on a stick, Domine."

"You should have them with you already," Timorous grumbled. "Grumio always had them ready."

Good old Grumio. Tully dumped the bucket and mop by the guards. Some water spilled from the bucket.

"Watch it!" said the guards' captain, who gave Tully a blow across the shoulders. "We don't want any of that filthy muck on our sandals."

Tully longed to pick up the bucket and throw the whole lot over him, but he restrained himself.

"Sorry," he mumbled.

"Hurry up!" Timorous shouted. "I need the sponge."

Tully wondered whether it would be worth paying for an amulet to wish for eagles to peck out the imperial family's livers daily.

🦆

Next stop was the changing room. This time, the beautiful mural painted on the wall showed Apollo the sun god, running a race with Mercury. The emperor and his cronies stripped off their togas and tossed them to the waiting slaves. The guards crowded in the room too. What with Timorous and his entourage, Tully and his burdens, the soldiers and the changing room slaves, there wasn't enough room to swing a siren.

"This is ridiculous!" barked Timorous. He pointed a finger at several of the guards in turn. "You, you and you, strip off and come with us to the exercise ground. The rest of you, clear off."

"But we've been ordered to stay with you…" protested the captain of the guards, an older man, his black hair touched with grey.

Timorous drew himself up and his face turned red. "I give you your orders. Who's emperor?" he shrieked.

It would have been funny, Timorous acting like a five-year-old if he hadn't been the emperor and capable of having anyone executed in a minute.

The captain stepped back immediately. "My apologies. Men, leave except the ones the emperor ordered to remain."

Tully couldn't help but notice that all the guards selected were tall, handsome ones. They slowly stripped off, not relishing this duty. Their lean bodies made the emperor and his friends look flabby and soft.

The emperor led the way out of the changing rooms, past the richly painted columns, to the exercise ground. The guards enjoyed playing ball until they realised they had to let the emperor win. Tully bet they wouldn't enjoy swimming with the emperor either.

He was looking at the swimming pool next to the exercise ground when he noticed bubbles trailing along the green water. That was odd because there wasn't anyone swimming in the pool.

"Swimming pool next," Timorous shouted.

They all started towards the pool.

Tully stood there for a moment, then dropped his tools and ran forward to make a grab for the emperor's toga.

"What the…?" shouted Timorous.

One of the naked guards tackled Tully, and they both fell heavily onto the mosaic floor.

Winded, Tully gasped, "Danger! The pool! Timorous!"

Luckily, the oaf who'd ploughed him over, heard his wheeze, and also shouted. "Danger!"

He had a much stronger bellow than Tully, and his shout reverberated around the exercise grounds. The others stopped short. At that moment, the water in the pool rippled then surged as an invisible something heaved itself out of the pool, spraying water, leaving puddles all around. They could see wet claw prints coming towards them.

As one, they all fled towards the changing rooms.

Just as they neared the entrance, a man screamed. Tully, despite himself, looked back and wished he hadn't. Postumus Flavius Stultus, older and fatter than the rest, had lagged behind the others. Something closed on his right leg and pulled him backwards. Blood gushed out, and a fountain of it fell onto an invisible creature, enough to show a long snout with dark brown muck smeared around the nostrils, massive jaws and beady eyes set close together. The creature dragged the howling senator this way and that for a few moments before he was tossed aside and lay there moaning.

Tully surged ahead into the changing room, pushing past the slaves clustered at the entrance.

"Get out of the way!" he shouted.

Tully looked around for weapons. The guards' swords! He picked one up and hefted it. Tully'd no idea how to use one. The blade felt unwieldy in his hands, as if he were winging round a leaden club… He looked back through the entrance.

More screams. The creature had caught another senator, Marcus Flavius Balbus. It trampled over his body to make straight for the emperor, who was staring at it over his shoulder and had foolishly slowed down.

Cursing, Tully dropped the sword and ran back out to grab the emperor and haul him along. He could hear the pound of the crocodile's feet at their heels. With a speed and strength that Tully didn't know he possessed, he lifted Timorous and charged into the changing rooms.

As Tully dropped Timorous, he jerked against Tully and sent him into the path of the crocodile. Its powerful jaws crunched down on his left arm. Tully screamed in agony. His right arm flailed around, looking for a weapon. His fingers found a strigil, the tool used for scraping oil. It should have been in the massage room, but Tully didn't care how it had got there. He clutched it. Such a puny weapon. How could he fight back against a creature with its own built-in armour plating? Its eyes!

He poked the crocodile in one of its beady eyes. It jerked and its jaws loosened. Tully pulled his arm out and away. It was throbbing, blood spurting from the bite marks.

A soldier grabbed a sword and jabbed at the crocodile's

other eye. His next jab made contact, and he rammed the sword in. The crocodile hissed and bellowed. The next second, it had vanished, and it left them staring at each other. Tully slid down to the floor, clutching his arm.

Timorous turned to the guard clutching the sword. "Well done, soldier. What's your name?"

"Flavius Actimus, Emperor," he said.

The other men crowded around him, clapping him on the back and congratulating him. No one thanked Tully. He wasn't the hero of the hour, he thought sourly. Of course not. He was just a slave.

"Report," Spectacula said. She sat on a high wooden chair that resembled a throne. Calpurnius and Lullius, her trusted freedmen, stood by her.

My arm hurts. She wouldn't care about that. Tully gave her an account of what had happened.

"Anything noteworthy?"

His being able to pick up and carry Timorous. Could it have been due to the swallow of ambrosia he'd had from Dero, the sea nymph's flagon when she'd rescued him and Nerites from that island? He certainly wasn't telling Spectacula about that.

"I noticed an old man loitering just as we arrived at the bathhouse. He seemed familiar, but it was only later I remembered he looked like one of the Jyptian slaves that was here recently. He was a magician who did tricks to amuse the ambassador. I didn't realise straightaway because he was hunched over and limping."

"Jyptian," Spectacula mused. "How interesting. Describe him as fully as you can."

Tully did his best. Tully hoped the Jyptian slave had magicked himself back to Jypt.

Lullius scribbled the details down on a wax tablet.

"Start people hunting for him straightaway," Spectacula ordered him. He bowed and left the room. "What else did you notice?"

"I'd the impression the crocodile wanted the emperor. It came straight for him, it tossed aside anyone else."

"Anything else?"

Tully hesitated but the dowager empress had a way of finding out things and if he didn't tell her but someone else did, it would be the worse for him. He plunged on. "The crocodile had excrement smeared around its nostrils and your son's body slave, Grumio, has been selling the imperial excrement."

"Did he say who he sold it to?"

"No, Domina. You'll have to ask him yourself." Tully felt bad for suggesting that. Grumio would be tortured. Slaves always were.

Her lips thinned. "No longer possible. Grumio died two hours ago."

Tully stared at her, shocked. Was that a coincidence or not?

Spectacula beckoned to Calpurnius, the fat one. "Give him one gold piece," she ordered.

Calpurnius shook out a piece from a leather bag lying on the desk and walked across to Tully. His damp hand pressed the coin into Tully's palm.

One measly gold coin for nearly getting killed and saving her precious son? And providing valuable information. He'd never save up enough to pay for his freedom at this rate.

"Thank you, Domina, you are too kind."

Spectacula's eyes narrowed, and she stood up. She'd detected his sarcasm. Tully took a trembling step back.

"I am kind, slave. Never forget, your continued existence depends on my continued benevolence." She made a shooing motion.

Tully scuttled from the chamber, his injured arm throbbing as he did so.

As Tully hurried away, someone bumped into him, right on his injured arm. He yelped with pain, stumbled and just managed to avoid knocking the bust of the Emperor Flatulus off its pedestal. There were too many statues lining the corridor, in his opinion.

"Tully! I'm so sorry. Did I hurt you?"

It was Melissa, Spectacula's handmaiden. Her dark eyes brimmed with concern as she took in his bandaged arm.

"It's nothing," muttered Tully, trying to act the brave soldier.

"I heard how brave you were from the changing room slaves," she said.

"You must mean Flavius Actimus," Tully said, scowling.

Her eyes widened. "No, I don't. You poked the monster's eye with a strigil. That's so much braver than doing it with a great big sword." She looked at him with admiration.

It might all be an act, although what reason had Melissa to flatter him? Tully felt his mouth curving into a smile. "Thank you."

"Keep safe and well, Tully. I must get back to my mistress."

She smiled at him, and Tully floated on air all the way back to the library.

🦆

Liz Tuckwell lives in London and shares her house with a husband and too many books. She enjoys reading and writing all types of fantasy, science fiction and horror. Liz also enjoys travelling when there isn't a pandemic. She's a member of the Clockhouse London Writers group and the British Fantasy Society.

Liz has had stories published in anthologies such as MCSI: Magical Crime Scene Investigation, Fairytales Punk'd, and in several of the Harvey Duckman Presents anthologies. She's also published two short story collections.

Find out more at www.liztuckwell.co.uk

SHAMBLE
A HOLLY TRINITY AND THE GHOSTS OF YORK STORY

BEN SAWYER

"Water hammer," he said, then waited for the clueless response on the other end of the line. "No, Mr Loschy, I'm absolutely positive. No, it's perfectly normal."

The plumber crouched beneath the bathroom sink, hands stroking the cool surface of the pipes, unaware of the burble of something powerful lurking behind the thin sheath of metal. His phone was wedged in the crook of his shoulder, and irritation at the day had long been brewing in his brain. And not just this day either. At his twisted angle, he could make out the bold red and purple of the To Let sign through the frosted glass. He still felt none the wiser about why there was a sash window beside the bath. Prospective residents clearly hoped to soak while their neighbours watched.

The man beneath the sink reassured the man on the end of the line, and indeed on the end of the sign, that all was well with the vacant property, and that his buy-to-let empire could gently expand unhindered by things he had little understanding of anyway.

"Water gets caught in the pipe that regulates pressure, and that's what causes all the banging," he explained while trying to manage the banging of the pressure regulator in his head. "Honestly, Mr Loschy, half the ghost stories you hear, that's what's really going on. It's all plumbing in the end."

Mr Loschy murmured his assent, accepting gracelessly that nothing stood between the terraced house and a profitable occupant. The plumber ended the call, and began packing up his things. That was when something rushed from the pipes to do its work.

Later that night, a vast shape crawled from the depths of a body of water many miles away, and began its long, deathly trudge to where its memories began.

When the plumber awoke, he was lying in the bath and three people had appeared in the bathroom with him. Beyond the sash, it was night. There were two women leaning over him, studying his face by torchlight. Behind them stood a tall elegant man in a suit. To his eyes, the man's face appeared green, which he put down to the dim light. When his awareness settled, he felt cold, chilled to the bone throughout his entire body. His hands and feet, he could barely feel at all.

"Please tell me you know what's going on here," the woman holding the torch said, while the other absent-mindedly toyed with her mess of shaggy curls.

"Don't ask me, I've already told you all I know," she replied in a thick York accent.

"Holly, all you said was 'I'm gonna have a barney with summat'," the first woman protested. "No clue as to what we're dealing with. Just that."

"It's not all spooky mysteries, you know," the one called Holly said, as if too much had already been asked of her. "There's not always stuff to figure out. Sometimes, some big ugly bastard just wants a barney, so out comes the magic sword. That's what's meant to be going on here."

She accentuated her point by rattling the blade slung at her hip. He wasn't surprised she had a sword, even though he should have been. People didn't carry swords. That wasn't normal. But he realised with mounting unease that he had been expecting one.

"Anyroad, I don't like it either, barneys are dead boring when you get two or three in a row," Holly continued. "And I have to walk back in whatever state I'm in. Bleeding all the way home with me backside in a sling. Not fun."

"So how does a dead guy in a bath figure into this… barney?" the first woman asked.

Holly leaned in closer, expelling a breath through pursed lips inches from his face.

"Dunno, really," she said. "I doubt I'm fighting him. He might be what's at stake, but barneys, they usually come down to summat wanting to smash the place up for its own sake."

He finally managed to force out a groan of breath that sent both women jumping back.

"Still alive," said Holly. "Wouldn't have thought he'd be up to that."

"Hi, can you hear me? It's alright, we're here to help." The first woman was smiling at him with genuine concern. It was meant to be comforting, but all it did was make him wonder what she was concerned about.

"Wha," he said, squeezing cold breaths from his lungs, each exhalation like regurgitating lumps of solid ice. "What's going on?"

"It's okay, we just found you," she continued softly. "We're going to try and get you out of here. Don't panic. My name's Mira. What's yours?"

"B," he began, spitting the hard sound over chilled lips. "B-B-B… Barney."

The two women exchanged a surprised look.

"That is a mad coincidence," Holly said.

"No, Holly," Mira said, gesturing back and forth between her friend and him. "You thought you were here for a barney, maybe you're actually here for Barney."

"No, I'm not!" Holly protested. "The only one using the word barney is me! Don't overthink this, it's just a monster fight, and, okay, we really should get him out of that stuff if he's gonna be alive…"

"Stuff?" he gasped, getting the word out in one go this time. His breathing quickened.

"Oh God, he doesn't know," Mira said. "Everything's going to be alright, Barney, just don't look down…"

He instinctively disobeyed, tilting his head as far forward as it could go, and felt a tiny tickling around his throat. His eyes looked down until they strained in their sockets and then he saw it.

The bath he lay in was filled to the brim with a tangle of dark green pond weeds. The foliage was bursting from the taps right where his feet were supposed to be, and smothering the body he could no longer feel. He screamed, pouring what little energy he had into the throaty yell, and as he did, his vision blurred, and he felt himself trudging down empty streets, coming closer, oh so slowly...

"...going to get you out of this!" Mira was saying as he found himself back in the bathroom.

"He did this to me!" Barney cried out. Stinging tears formed in the corners of his eyes, lone dots of warmth in the smothering cold.

"You know who did this?" asked Holly, leaning in with renewed interest.

"Him!" shouted Barney, glaring at the other figure in the room. "The green bloke!"

"What green bloke?" Holly said, and he knew with horror that she had no idea the green-faced man was even there, lurking silently behind them, soaking up every moment as he waited to bind them in leaves of their own...

Barney gestured as violently as he could with just his head. Mira turned in the direction he was looking, dropped the torch in shock, then snatched up an object from the floor to protect herself with. It was only then that Holly noticed the green man.

"Abandinus!" she said. "Mira, put that down, it's alright, he's a mate! How long have you been stood there?"

"Oh, I got here first," the green man said with a broad smile. "You were very occupied with your discussion. Greetings, Mountain. And this must be the estimable Mira Chaudhri. My cousins told me of your last encounter."

"Who is he?" Mira asked nervously, still grasping her improvised weapon, which Barney now made out through the shadows as an umbrella. Why an umbrella? The questions were building up like weeds on… Before he could complete the thought, he drifted again. This time he could feel the soles of his feet, grinding roughly across coarse ground. When he awoke, the green man leaned in close with a broad smile on his oily face and blinked two big, round, fishy blinks.

"…a river spirit," Holly was explaining to Mira like that was another everyday thing. "He don't mean no harm. Although, now I think, there is a bloke covered in duckweed, which don't look good for him. I'm not here for a barney with you lot, am I?"

"I thought you were mates?" Mira said.

"We are," Holly replied. "Just sort of on a clock. Tell me it's not that time already."

"Oh no, not yet," Abandinus said with a genial smile. "I assure you we did not do this either. I'm merely here because water takes an interest in water."

Cool fingers rested on Barney's forehead, as Abandinus closed his eyes and breathed heavily.

"Ah yes," he said. "Shamble. Well, I suppose time was due."

"What's Shamble?" Holly demanded.

"A more ancient spirit of the water than I," Abandinus said. "I suspect you will find a sealed well in the foundations of this house. That's usually how this begins."

"How what begins?" Mira asked, gripping her umbrella all the tighter.

"Offerings made in thanks to a water source draw a creature that thrives on them," Abandinus explained. "Like myself. But then people stop using the water, stop making the offerings, and resentments build up. Usually, the creature drifts away. But if the anger won't drain, it must rush forth."

"I'll check the basement for metaphors," Holly said, but Abandinus dismissed her words with a languid wave of his hand.

"The well will be sealed," he said. "Shamble will have moved on, through the waters underground. He goes to where humans drink, hoping they'll think it's his gift. If no one is using the well, he will have gone to what they use instead."

"But there won't be any offerings, wherever he goes," Mira said. "People haven't done that for centuries. They know where their water comes from."

"Do you know where your water comes from?" Abandinus asked with a sly smile.

"Okay, no, but I know who I have to pay for it," she replied after a dumbfounded moment.

"He walks…" Barney gasped, as he felt the body that was not his, and yet somehow was, moving in great lumbering steps. He saw the terraced houses on either side of him, and in the distance, a splash of purple and red that told the world this place was open. This place wanted people. People wanted water, and would be grateful. Once they'd learned respect…

"He walks," Mira said, then looked to the taps. "This all came through the pipes, the pipes come from… look, I don't know what happens in between, but is he walking all the way to this house from the reservoir?"

"To punish the city that ignored him with flood and horror," Abandinus said, flicking a sideways glance in Holly's direction. "Luckily, this particular city has a household god to protect it."

"Yay me!" she said sarcastically. "Told you this'd end in a barney. Speaking of Barney, what's his deal?"

Barney felt his head throbbing, as one horrific revelation built up on another, apocalyptic imagery thrown about as casually as he might discuss central heating. And he knew the worst was to come. Even as he felt himself sucked into their talk of gods and monsters, he could not forget he was in this bath for a reason, and he knew that reason could not be good.

"Water always needs to flow," Abandinus said, pitilessly. "Through rivers and streams and the gaps in the Earth, or through the passages your people make. Shamble will need a vessel if he is to have a physical presence to enact his rage. He needs…"

"Plumbing," Mira said sourly. "Barney is plumbing."

They were all looking at him, and he felt them blur across his vision. He looked down onto the black polished roof of a van, a glossy surface he towered over. He saw the face reflected back at him under the moon, a mass of leaves and weeds in tangled growths. Fear filled him and he roared in response, a great round lamprey mouth of spiralling teeth and steaming breath cycling outwards. He wanted to lash out and saw an arm culminating in a tube of rusted iron encrusted with dark, stained ice. The limb swung…

A rumbling noise and the crunching of breaking metal snapped Barney back to the bathroom. It had clearly startled his rescuers as well, who looked from one to another in mounting horror.

"It's here," Holly said to Mira. "Give us the brolly. Look after him."

As Holly and Abandinus strode out of the room, Mira leaned over Barney and yanked open the sash. She leapt back with a start at what she saw.

Barney twisted in his grave of weeds, determined to know what was happening, and saw the thing whose reflection he had glimpsed. A lumbering, hunched shape, some ten feet tall and nearly as wide, walked, no, *shambled* with painful steps up the street. Its body was a mound of green foliage, with pipes of different materials thrusting outwards from its curved broad back – wood and copper and iron, some bright and shining, others gnarled and corroded. Its right arm trailed behind it, dragging that terrible hunk of ice with a grinding noise across the concrete. Barney saw that Mira had her phone in her hand and looked terrified.

"Holly?" she said. "Are you seeing what I'm seeing?"

Barney felt his mind drift, felt his vision slip into the eyes of the creature. Holly and Abandinus stood before it in the middle of the street, tiny adversaries pulsing with blood and water in the face of its immensity.

"Yeah, Mira, could not really miss that," Holly was saying, her voice ululating as if underwater. "He's a big'un. And he's got a water hammer. Nice touch that."

"...out of there, he's going to kill you!" Mira was yelling when Barney returned to his own body. "No, don't you dare... Holly!"

A rushing roar filled the enclosed space of the bathroom. Barney looked out of the window and saw blasts of steam surging from the pipes that encrusted the creature's body. He flinched as a cloud of warm vapour drifted through the open window, and then he became the monster once again. Holly drew her sword, the umbrella wielded like a second weapon in her left hand. Abandinus stood beside her, hands in pockets. One face was fierce, the other gently amused.

"Don't suppose you've got a plan," Holly said.

"I do indeed," Abandinus replied, before Barney was pulled back to himself. He saw Mira tearing uselessly at the weeds that covered him. The leaves just reformed around every opening she made.

"Come on!" she shouted, as Barney slipped again into the monster's mind and tasted its rage. To his surprise, Holly was not paying attention to it. Instead, she was yelling at a goose that was standing right where Abandinus had previously been.

"…little flappy scutting bastard!" she shouted. "You can't just exposit and bugger off!"

"This is not our battle," the goose said calmly in Abandinus' voice. "Good fighting, Mountain."

The transformed river spirit flapped its wings, hissed loudly, and flew away.

"I hope someone feeds you bread till your guts blow out your arsehole!" Holly shouted after the departing water fowl. "And not nice bread neither! Stale!"

She turned, and looked up. Her sword clattered to the road as a roar built up in Barney's throat and…

Barney was back in the bath and a thundering bellow shook the house. Steam flooded through the open window, warm across his chilled face. He became the creature again and saw the steam he had vented from his maw dispersing to reveal a round black shape, its surface slick and shiny with moisture, vapour rising from the edges and the puddles that surrounded it. Holly stood up from where she had crouched behind her open umbrella, and took up the sword she had dropped.

"Righty-ho then," she snarled. "You are so getting flushed."

He saw her darting in his direction, so tiny next to his vast bulk, saw the blade flash in front of him, felt ice and vines knitting across the cuts it made. His shoulder rolled in a thunderous arc, the weight of the water hammer crashing to the ground, ice cracking and refreezing under the impact. Holly rolled away from the blow, then again.

He vented steam at her and she dived clear. The water hammer rose for another strike.

"Water hammer…" he breathed, catching Mira's attention as the bathroom swung back into his field of vision. He could hear the howling of the beast outside, and the tiny shouts of exertion as Holly battled it.

"What did you say?" Mira said. "Water hammer, what is that? Holly said it had a water hammer, what does that mean?"

"Water caught in the pipe," he gasped, as the roaring began to fill his head. "Have to drain the… ta…"

And then he was gone again, back into the battle, flinging blows made to crush and blasts of boiling fluid. His jaw distended, opening wide in a swirling vortex of jagged edges to consume her. She sprinted away, lashing at his hip. There was no pain. Nothing could stop him taking his rightful place if only…

Barney flinched and was himself again. Mira was spinning the taps and yanking on the vines dangling from them. More and more weed came flooding into the bath, slick and wet and smelling of decay. The more of it that came, the looser it felt around him. His arms were numb from stillness, but he could roll himself from side to side at least. A bellow roared out of the street. Barney lurched until his head pushed out through the window and saw the creature. Its great round mouth howled at the sky as steam billowed from every pipe of its body. Leaves fell away and were swept up into a tornado of tattered greenery and boiling mist. The pipes themselves began to flake and shatter, rotten fragments joining the tumult. As the connection between Shamble and Barney withered in the house's pipes, the leaves blew into the sky. By the time, Mira had hauled him from the bath, nothing remained.

Barney walked home in the gathering morning. It had taken some time for feeling to return to his legs. They had stayed with him, Mira trying her best to comfort him, Holly slumped on the floor, clearly even more exhausted than he was.

"I don't know how I'm gonna explain all this," he had said. It had only just occurred to him that he had accepted a man turning into a goose without a second thought. Things were so strange he had taken the merely bizarre in his stride.

"You won't have to," Mira had told him. "The neighbours will all have slept through the whole thing. It's what happens. Even when someone's having a barney with a giant monster."

"Okay, this one weren't just a barney." Holly had snapped upright from a doze. "I'd totally have won if it was."

When Barney thought of that moment, he feared for the fearless woman. He remembered that she had barely scratched the creature. But she had tried, so hard. This was what they did, he realised. These were the people who fixed things he could never imagine. That seemed like the best way to view it. Mira had said as much.

"I can't get my head round this. I really can't."

"Don't try to," Mira had explained. "Just… try something normal for a bit. It helps. Trust me, I get through every night with her because I get to go home afterwards."

He idly wondered who was waiting for Mira to come home, because it seemed to him very likely that one day she wouldn't. The thought saddened him, but brought forth a flush of admiration too. Holly was merely fearless, but Mira was *brave*.

"Sitting right here," came a jokey protest from a virtually recumbent Holly. "She's probably right though. Can't say I know what normal is, but it seems to keep her coming back whenever I need her."

"Which was tonight," Mira pointed out.

"Which is a lot of nights," Holly smiled a sleepy smile. "Brains of the outfit, that's you."

That was when he had left, but before he cleared the room, Mira had one last lesson to impart.

"I don't know anything about plumbing. But we beat it because you did. I don't know if that helps, but… plumbing. It's a thing."

Barney smiled as the sun came up again, and felt that he had somehow contributed to its ascent. His phone was buzzing in his pocket, and he had no idea how long it had been doing so. He answered with a grin.

"Barney Williams, subcontractor to the maintenance crew of the universe," he said, then allowed normal to embrace him once again. It was all plumbing in the end.

Ben Sawyer is a writer of paranormal fiction who has lived in and around York for 15 years. This ancient and absurdly haunted city has grown very close to his heart, so he decided to take a funhouse mirror to its dark snickelways. The first Holly Trinity novel, Holly Trinity and the Ghosts of York, was published in 2021. He is currently working on a sequel.

Find out more at: bensawyerauthor.wordpress.com

Also available from Sixth Element Publishing
in paperback and eBook:

Harvey Duckman Presents… Volume 1
Published April 2019
*including stories by: Kate Baucherel,
D.W. Blair, A.L. Buxton, R. Bruce Connelly,
Joseph Carrabis, Nate Connor, Marios Eracleous,
Craig Hallam, C.G. Hatton, Mark Hayes,
Peter James Martin, Reino Tarihmen, J.L. Walton,
Graeme Wilkinson and Amy Wilson.*

www.6epublishing.net

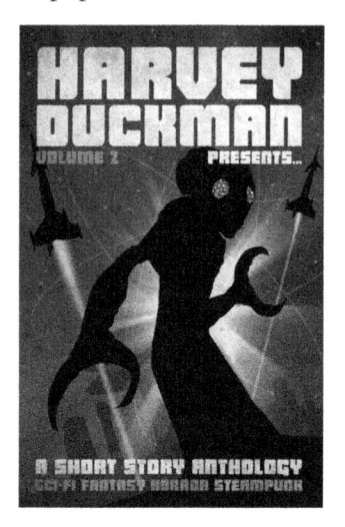

Also available from Sixth Element Publishing
in paperback and eBook:

Harvey Duckman Presents… Volume 2
Published July 2019
*including stories by: Phil Busby, A.L. Buxton,
J.S. Collyer, R. Bruce Connelly, Phoebe Darqueling,
Lynne Lumsden Green, Craig Hallam, Jon Hartless,
Mark Hayes, Andy Hill, Fred Johnson, Peter James Martin,
Ben McQueeney and A.D. Watts.*

www.6epublishing.net

Also available from Sixth Element Publishing
in paperback and eBook:

Harvey Duckman Presents… Volume 3
Published October 2019
*including stories by: Peter James Martin, Ben McQueeney,
A.L. Buxton, R. Bruce Connelly, Phoebe Darqueling,
Melissa Wuidart Phillips, Marios Eracleous, Nate
Connor, James Porter, Joseph Carrabis, Cheryllynn Dyess,
Erudessa Gentian, Liz Tuckwell, JL Walton and Amy Wilson,
as well as a bonus 'Harvey Duckman' story by Mark Hayes,
and a foreword by Craig Hallam.*

www.6epublishing.net

Also available from Sixth Element Publishing
in paperback and eBook:

**Harvey Duckman Presents…
Christmas Special 2019**
Published December 2019
*including stories by: Thomas Gregory, Andy Hill,
Peter James Martin, Craig Hallam, Kate Baucherel,
Cheryllynn Dyess, Marios Eracleous, Zack Brooks,
Ben McQueeney, Maggie Kraus, Gerald Wiley,
Lynne Lumsden Green, Mark Hayes,
Ben Sawyer and R. Bruce Connelly.*

www.6epublishing.net

Also available from Sixth Element Publishing
in paperback and eBook:

Harvey Duckman Presents... Volume 4
Published March 2020
including stories by: Adrian Bagley, Crysta K Coburn, Thomas Gregory, Christine King, Peter James Martin, John Holmes-Carrington, A.L. Buxton, Zack Brooks, Fred Johnson, Ben McQueeney, Keld Hope, Deborah Barwick, Jon Hartless, R. Bruce Connelly, and Mark Hayes, as well as a bonus 'Harvey Duckman' story by Andy Hill, and a foreword by Amy Wilson.

www.6epublishing.net

Also available from Sixth Element Publishing in paperback and eBook:

Harvey Duckman Presents… Volume 5
Published July 2020
including stories by: Adrian Bagley, Kate Baucherel, A.L. Buxton, Aidan Cairnie, Joseph Carrabis, R. Bruce Connelly, Tony Harrison, Mark Hayes, Scott Howard, Peter James Martin, Alex Minns, Andrew Openshaw, Melissa Rose Rogers, Kathrine Machon and Liz Tuckwell, with a foreword from fantasy author Ben McQueeney.

www.6epublishing.net

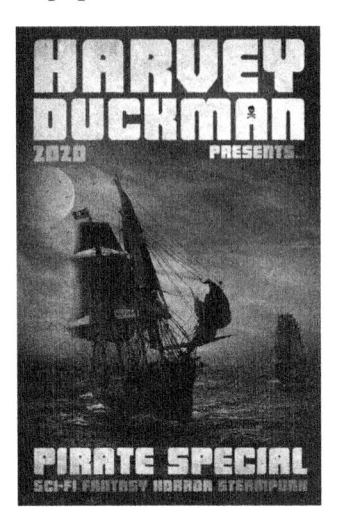

Also available from Sixth Element Publishing
in paperback and eBook:

Harvey Duckman Presents… Pirate Special 2020
Published September 2020
*includes stories by: Amy Wilson, Ben Sawyer,
Kate Baucherel, Mark Hayes, Melissa Wuidart
Phillips, C.G. Hatton, A.L. Buxton, Reino Tarihmen,
Liz Tuckwell, R. Bruce Connelly, Mark Sayeh,
Christine King, Joseph Carrabis, Loïc Baucherel,
Nils Nisse Visser, Peter James Martin and Andy Hill.*

www.6epublishing.net

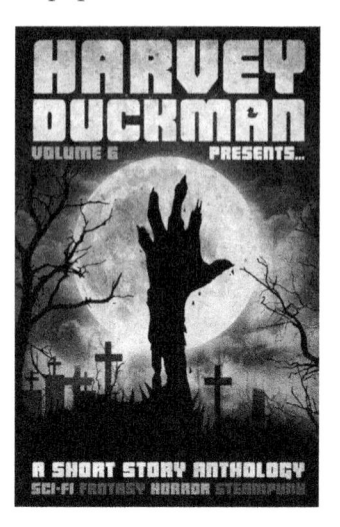

Also available from Sixth Element Publishing
in paperback and eBook:

Harvey Duckman Presents… Volume 6
Published December 2020
*includes stories by: Andy Hill, J.A. Wood, Mark Hayes,
R. Bruce Connelly, A.D. Watts, Liz Tuckwell,
Ben McQueeney, Melissa Wuidart Phillips, J.S. Collyer,
Peter James Martin, C. K. Roebuck, Joseph Carrabis,
Alexandrina Brant, Tony Harrison and D.T. Langdale,
with a foreword from steampunk author Jon Hartless.*

www.6epublishing.net

Also available from Sixth Element Publishing in paperback and eBook:

Harvey Duckman Presents… Volume 7
Published March 2021
includes stories by: Will Nett, Jeshanth KS, John Holmes-Carrington, Tamara Clelford, Dominic JP Nelson-Ashley, Peter James Martin, Kate Baucherel, Andrew Openshaw, Graeme Wilkinson, Marios Eracleous, R. Bruce Connelly, Robin Moon, Ross Steven Pickering, Mark Hayes and Joseph Carrabis, with a foreword from Andy Hill.

www.6epublishing.net

Also available from Sixth Element Publishing
in paperback and eBook:

Harvey Duckman Presents… Volume 8
Published September 2021
includes stories by: Christine King, Mark Hayes, Alex Minns, Muriel R. Blythman, Adrian Bagley, Crysta K. Coburn, Peter James Martin, Joseph Carrabis, Jack Pentire, R. Bruce Connelly, Melissa Wuidart Phillips, Davia Sacks, Liz Tuckwell, Kate Baucherel and Alexandrina Brant, with a foreword from CG Hatton.

www.6epublishing.net

Find Harvey on Facebook:
www.facebook.com/harveyduckman

Find Harvey on Twitter:
twitter.com/DuckmanHarvey

Harvey Duckman Presents… is edited by C.G. Hatton

C.G. Hatton is the author of the fast-paced, military science fiction books set in the high-tech Thieves' Guild universe of galactic war and knife-edge intrigue. She has a PhD in geology and a background in journalism, and is currently working on the ninth book in the Thieves' Guild series, as well as compiling and editing more volumes of Harvey Duckman Presents…

Find out more at www.cghatton.com

•

www.harveyduckman.com

Printed in Great Britain
by Amazon